She's
PROMISED TO HIM
BUT I HAVE HER
HEART

3

A NOVEL BY

VIVIAN BLUE

Royalty Publishing House is now accepting manuscripts from aspiring or experienced urban romance authors!

WHAT MAY PLACE YOU ABOVE THE REST:

Heroes who are the ultimate book bae: strong-willed, maybe a little rough around the edges but willing to risk it all for the woman he loves.

Heroines who are the ultimate match: the girl next door type, not perfect - has her faults but is still a decent person. One who is willing to risk it all for the man she loves.

The rest is up to you! Just be creative, think out of the box, keep it sexy and intriguing!

If you'd like to join the Royal family, send us the first 15K words (60 pages) of your completed manuscript to submissions@royaltypublishing-house.com

I would like to dedicate this series to my loving cousin Stanley Antonio "KTone" Sparkling. You were so happy and amped when I first got published. You always gave me loads of encouragement and support, cousin, and I love you so much for that! It has not been the same since you've been gone. Every time I walk up Mama's steps, I look over at your van then the house and expect you to come out and say, "What's up, cousin?" Then you flash that infamous smile. I will never be the same, cousin, but your memory will live on! Another piece of me has left, but you will live through your seeds, and we will never forget you! #LongLiveK-Tone—the Mayor of the Ville! (Still crying mad tears!)

ACKNOWLEDGMENTS

I would like to thank God for giving me this gift of writing. It is a blessing to be able to share my stories with you guys, and I appreciate each and every one of you that come along on my adventures! This book is different from what I've written in the past, and I've enjoyed pushing myself to create this wonderful love story. It is difficult to understand the customs and beliefs of other religions when you don't have the knowledge needed to do so. We should never judge a book by its cover, not unless you know the information that's inside. I have had experience in making a decision to convert to a religion that was unfamiliar to me for love, and it was something that helped me discover how powerful the meaning of the word was in my life. I hope you enjoyed this story, and thank you for always rocking with me!

Also, I would like to thank the love of my life that gave me the inspiration to write this story. William Maurice Kemper, AKA Kamose, I will forever love and be grateful to you for helping me become the person I am spiritually. I only wish we were able to further our journey into this crazy thing called love, but we will be together inshallah! Continue to Rest in Peace! XoXo

I would like to thank my publisher, Porscha Sterling, for believing in me and giving me the opportunity to put my thoughts out here in the world! Also, I would like to thank you for reaching out to check on me. It shows how much you care and that mother hen is always watching over her flock. I am truly grateful to you and the Royalty Publishing House Family for all of your love and support! I would like to give a special shout out to Michelle Davis for all of her help and support! You have really been a huge support to me with my transitions and the development of my craft. You and Porscha want Royalty authors to win, and both of you are giving us so much more than people realize. You guys are true mentors and help so much with helping us become better writers. I've come to understand that Michelle is a major gear in this crazy machine that keeps us shining, and I want you to know that I appreciate you! (XoXo.)

I can't forget my editor, Katrice Crawford! We've started this new literary relationship, and I appreciate the fact that you get me! To Latisha Smith Burns and her editing team at Touch of Class Publishing Services: "Where class meets perfection!", you are truly gems, and I appreciate all of the love and support that you give me! You have always gotten my oddness, and I am so grateful that you do! You have been a great mentor and support to me, and I love you madly!

To my test reader, LaShonda "Shawny" Jennings, thank you for your input and "realness!" You give me my reality check, and I appreciate the love and support! I am thankful to all of my readers for being a part of my literary career because you keep me hopeful, humble, and hungry to give you my very best work! To my readers, thank you! Thank you! Thank you! You guys are rock stars, and I am truly grateful to you! You're the real MVPs!

Peace, Love & Blessings

Synopsis

Nika and Usian secretly got married, but not everyone is happy about it. Subira uses this as a way to show her family that they have no control over her daughter's life, and Nika shows them that what she feels in her heart is more important than the deceitful arranged marriage that everyone wants her to go through. However, Nika's family aren't the only ones who are outraged about the marriage. Jessica is devasted by the news and refuses to accept the fact that Usian is done with her.

CJ is stressed out, trying to hide Precious's pregnancy from his uncle, not to mention he's lied to Usian about Precious's involvement in the robbery. Pooh is steady applying pressure, and CJ knows that he has to do something about it, especially since he killed his mother. CJ should have been handled this situation, and if he's not careful, things can get even worse.

Relationships will be put to the test, and loyalties will fall where they lie. The love that Usian and Nika share is unwavering, but even perfect relationships face adversity. Will they be able to overcome everything that's coming their way, or will the hate and pressure being applied to the both of them be the cause of their downfall?

A Month Ago…

"*W*hat is taking her so long?" Nika complained, pacing back and forth. "She said it would only take a few minutes, but it seems like it's taking forever."

"Calm down, Nika. Your ass gon' get some dick," Kimmie replied, chuckling. "That nigga put that fat ass rock on your finger earlier. Now you're ready to fall on the dick!"

Nika cut her eyes at Kimmie then laughed out loud. She had only been married to Usian for six hours, but she couldn't wait for the moment of truth to happen. She was anxiously horny and ready to be deflowered by her husband, and things were taking too long. The moment they said their I do's, Nika wanted to go into the broom closet and pull Usian's dick out. "Are you sure you're ready for this?" Kimmie asked frankly.

"Yes, I'm ready for it! I've been waiting for months to have Usian take my virginity. I'm surprised he didn't suck my virginity away, the way he pushes his tongue in and out of my little girl," Nika said, laughing. "I've experienced countless orgasms from him sodomizing me."

"Don't use that word, girl! It sounds like he's a sexual predator or something."

"Really, Kimmie?" Nika asked, rolling her eyes. "You know what I mean."

1

"Yeah, I know what you mean. He can sexual predator all over that pu—"

"You are so immature," Nika interrupted, walking over to the dressing mirror.

Subira had rented a suite for Nika and Usian to spend their wedding night. They went to the mosque on Grand and Cass Avenue and had a small ceremony. There were only a few close friends and family members in attendance. On Usian's side, his mother Jackie, both nephews, CJ and Jordan, Mac, Whisper, and his wife, Big Lee, were there. Nika had only her mother, auntie Meme, and her husband Hanif, Zaida, and Kimmie there with her. Subira made Zaida swear on her life that she wouldn't tell anyone about the wedding. Subira had plans on how she wanted to present her daughter and her new son-in-law to everyone, and it had a lot of shock and awe involved.

Subira had made both of their wedding garments from some of the finest fabrics she had brought back from Africa the last time she had gone for a visit. She anticipated that Nika would be getting married soon, and she wanted to be prepared when the time arrived. She figured Nika would want to go to a bridal shop to purchase her wedding gown, but to her surprise, Nika asked her mother to make her dress. It was a simple white A-line dress that had white lace embroidered details on the bodice, neck, sleeves, and hem of the gown. It had long sleeves and a high collar that flowed all the way down to her feet. Nika wanted to follow the tradition and cover her entire body, and she even opted to wear a white and gold embroidered hijab with two diamond circles that hung in the center of her forehead. Her makeup was simple and elegant. She put a little white shadow on her eyelids, along with a little mascara and some lip gloss. Nika was beautiful, so she didn't need all of the extras. Besides, Usian always complained when she put on makeup, so she wanted to please him. Subira even made Usian a Thobe, which was a long robe worn by Muslim men. It was made from the same white fabric as Nika's gown, and it had the same white embroidery around the neck, the cuffs of the sleeves, and the bottom hem. Also, she made him a pair of loose-fitting pants that he wore underneath, and he covered his head with a kufi that mimicked her hijab. Usian decided to order himself and Nika a pair of white red bottoms to go with their wedding attire. He bought her a pair of white pumps and himself a pair of white loafers. Men were expected to dress modestly like women in Islam, and the Quran addressed this for both sexes.

"I hope I don't disappoint Usian tonight." Nika cried, sitting down on the edge of the bed.

She and Kimmie were in the room where Subira would be staying the night. There was a certain order of business that needed to be verified, and Subira required it to be done immediately like they did back home in Africa. Soon as the deed was done, Usian was to bring her proof that Nika was in fact a virgin.

"You're being silly, friend," Kimmie told Nika, sitting down next to her. "You're a virgin, so it can't be bad—not unless his dick doesn't fit. However, I want to warn you that it's going to hurt."

"Hurt!" Nika shouted, looking nervous. "No one said anything about pain!"

"Calm your ass down!" Kimmie said, getting up off the bed. "I already told you that it hurt the first few times I did it after I lost my virginity."

She walked over to the dresser where her purse was sitting. She picked it up and started digging around in it, looking for her magic wand. They couldn't smoke a blunt in the room, but they could smoke on her vape pen and get the same high. "Viola!" Kimmie shouted, holding up her vape. "Here is the solution to your anxiety!"

Kimmie sashayed back over to the bed and handed Nika the vape. She sat back down next to her and smiled with self-satisfaction.

"Good answer!" Nika agreed, putting it to her lips and taking a hit.

She held the smoke in her mouth for a few seconds before blowing it out. A harsh cough came behind it, and her eyes watered.

"Damn, Nika! I told you to hit it, not fill both lungs up with smoke," Kimmie said, taking the pen from her.

"I didn't—"*cough... cough*—"mean to hit it that hard," Nika uttered, still coughing. "I need another hit of that tho'."

"What you need to do is calm the fuck down," Kimmie declared. "It's really no big deal, Nika. Usian is experienced, so he should know how to distract you from the pain. Plus, you get to test your dick-sucking skills tonight!"

Kimmie pumped her arms up in the air and celebrated. "I know I've taught you how to suck dick like a porn star with those popsicles to practice on while watching the entire catalogue of *Big Black Bad Bitches Suck A Mean Dick Volumes 1-25*. Usian is going to be so surprised, and I bet he'll swear up and down that you've sucked dick before."

"But I don't want him to think that, Kimmie."

"Bitch, don't worry... I'm being facetious," Kimmie assured her. "Your ass is going to fuck up as soon as you put the dick to your lips, but it's all good, girl!"

"You know what, Kimmie? Fuck you!" Nika replied, snatching the vape out of Kimmie's hand. She took a hit of the vape and held the smoke in.

"Don't get mad at me because you're going to freeze up when it's time to suck that big dick!" Kimmie teased.

"How do you know that Usian's dick is big?" Nika questioned, raising an eyebrow.

"Girl, please! Usian is always walking around in gray jogging pants, and he walks like his nuts are heavy," Kimmie stated, frankly. "You know a nigga got a big dick by the way they walk, and Usian walks like his dick is in the way."

Nika burst into laughter, while Kimmie got up and mocked the way Usian walked. Her silliness was taking Nika's mind off the fact that losing her virginity was going to be painful. It was a much-needed distraction at a very stressful time. Nika's phone dinged, alerting her that she had a text message. She hoped that it was her mother saying she was on her way down to get her, but it was a message from Roc.

Roc: I don't know what the fuck is up with you, Nika but you better be ready to get married after Ramadan! I've put up with your bullshit for far too long and it is time that you act your age and take responsibility of your obligations. Your father wanted you to have your husband selected, and I was the choice that Jumba made! I will give you space for the holy month, but as soon as it is over, I expect you to be ready and available to me!

Nika read the message and instantly got disgusted. This nigga really had life messed up, and Nika wanted to tell him to go to hell. She was already married to the man who had her heart, and she couldn't wait to throw it up in his face, but until then, Nika would play the game like it was supposed to be played. She'd have her day to make that nigga cry, and

Usian was going to make sure it happened. She sent Roc a simple text to sum up her feelings.

Nika: Nigga fuck you!

"Who is that, texting you?" Kimmie asked nosily.

"Nobody important," Nika said, placing her phone down beside her.

The Purple Haze in the vape was starting to get her right. She had a nice buzz forming, but the butterflies in her stomach were still dancing around. Nika took another hit of the vape when Subira walked into the room.

"Are you ready, my child?" Subira asked, walking over to Nika.

"About as ready as I'm going to be," Nika replied apprehensively.

"You don't sound sure, baby. Is everything okay?" Subira asked, concerned. She stood in front of Nika and studied her face for a moment. "You look absolutely beautiful in your night gown and robe," Subira complimented.

"Thank you, Mama. You have really good taste," Nika replied, smiling.

"Did you put the other stuff on up under the gown?" Subira asked, lifting an eyebrow.

"Yes, ma'am," Nika replied. "I figured being naked up under my gown would be enough, but you told me to put everything on, so I did."

"Being naked is fine, but you want to entice your husband," Subira advised. "You want to make a show out of revealing yourself to him. You are offering him a very important gift, baby. Your virginity is the most precious gift you could give your husband, next to his first-born child. Usian is a very worthy man, and I'm so happy that the two of you came to your senses!"

Tears filled Subira's eyes as she reached out and touched Nika's cheek. Nika was already filled with a lot of emotion, and a lone tear ran down her cheek. Subira wiped it away with her hand before kissing the middle of Nika's forehead.

"I love you, Mama," Nika said, grabbing her mother's hand.

She kissed the inside of her palm before placing it over her heart.

"I love you too, sweet girl," Subira replied.

"And I love both of y'all." Kimmie cried, wiping the tears from her eyes.

Both Nika and Subira looked over at her and smiled.

"We love you too, Kimmie," Nika said, reaching out her hand.

Kimmie walked over and hugged her friend. "And thank you for everything. I couldn't have made it through this day without you."

"I agree," Subira said, placing her hand on Kimmie's cheek. "You've been a very good friend to my daughter, and I appreciate you."

"Thanks, Ms. Subira. That means a lot," Kimmie replied, wiping tears away.

"Well, baby girl, are you ready to go to your husband and become a woman?" Subira asked, smiling.

"I like the sound of that," Nika gloated. "And yes... I'm ready to go be with my husband."

Nika hit the vape one last time while Kimmie sang "Tonight is the Night" by Betty White. She handed it to Kimmie while holding in the smoke. She closed her eyes and counted to twenty then let out the smoke slowly.

"Let us pray before I take you upstairs," Subira suggested. "We need to ask Allah to guide you and Usian because I want a grandbaby in nine months."

"Mama!" Nika called out. "Can I at least be married for a year before you start asking for grandchildren? I want to enjoy my husband by myself for a while."

"A mother can dream and pray for what she wants without the consent of their child," Subira mentioned, rolling her eyes. "However, I will pray for love, respect, loyalty... Oh, and fertility!"

USIAN WAS SITTING on the love seat, anxiously awaiting Subira to bring Nika to him. She had left after praying over him with Jackie to go get his bride. He couldn't wait to see Nika, but more importantly, he couldn't wait to get in between her thighs. They had been apart for the last two hours because Subira wanted to bathe Nika and prepare her for their wedding night. He understood that Nika was a virgin, and Subira wanted to make sure that her daughter was aware of what was going to take place in their wedding bed. Usian knew that Nika was fully aware, but he couldn't tell

Subira that. He'd been playing with her kitty for a while and had close, personal conversations with it. However, tonight would be different for the both of them. He was now able to do the one thing he so desired, but a bit of nervousness started to set in. It had been years since Usian had taken anyone's virginity, and to be doing it in his thirties felt weird. Also, he wasn't sure if he wanted to let Nika suck his dick. She was inexperienced, and sometimes, the not-so-skilled had a tendency to use their teeth in a not-so-good way. Usian knew that he would have to teach Nika how to please him, but could he be selfish and be the only one doing all of the pleasuring? A smile came across his face while he thought about the first time he'd gotten intimate with Nika. It was the day in the basement when she was on the washing machine, masturbating. She looked so good, sitting there, playing in between her legs, and Usian knew at that moment that Nika would be his woman.

"Why are you sitting over there with that silly smile on your face?" Jackie asked nosily.

"What you mean?" Usian asked nonchalantly.

"I said what I meant. You're sitting over there with a big ass smile on your face while staring off in a daze."

"Can't a brother be happy? I mean, I just married the perfect woman, and now I'm waiting to bust that—"

"Watch yo'self, Usian," Jackie warned, pointing at him.

"I'm playing, Mama," Usian replied, laughing. "I wasn't going to say the word."

"I don't know what the fuck is going to come out of your mouth sometimes," Jackie confessed. "I know you better watch your mouth though!"

"Yes, ma'am."

Usian laughed as he looked down at his phone. He had gotten a string of text messages from Jessica, and he couldn't figure out why she was texting him. She'd left a message in his DM and even inboxed him on Facebook. "I don't know why this girl is hitting me up like she's crazy or something," Usian complained.

"Who are you talking about?"

"Jessica. She's been hitting me up for the past two hours, and I don't know why. I been told her that I was cool on her ass so she needs to kick rocks."

"Jessica was thirsty," Jackie said, rolling her eyes. "I never thought she was good for you."

"You don't like nobody, Ma."

"That's not true," Jackie said defensively. "I like Amanika."

Usian looked at his mother and smiled.

"I like her too," Usian agreed, lifting his eyebrows up and down.

There was a knock at the door, and Usian sat straight up. He knew it was Subira bringing Nika to him, and he was ready to receive his bride. Jackie got up from the couch and walked over to the door. She looked back at Usian before opening the door and smiled warmly at her son. She turned the knob and pulled the door open to greet Subira and her new daughter-in-law.

"Oh! I wasn't aware that she was going to be dressed like this. Is she a ghost or some shit?" Jackie uttered, moving out of the way.

"In our religion, women are supposed to be completely covered, and their husbands are the only ones who are supposed to see them uncovered," Subira explained, walking into the room.

Nika followed closely behind Subira and giggled when Jackie made her statement. Nika was completely covered from head to toe in a white hijab that covered her complete face and body. The only thing they could see were her eyes, and they were big, brown, and very expressive. Subira didn't want anyone looking at her daughter while they went to the suite. Nika was for Usian's eyes only, and Subira was going to make sure that it was done properly.

"Usian, I have brought you your wife," Subira expressed happily.

"Yo' wife is here, nig—"

"Nika!" Subira said sternly.

"I mean... husband, I am here to please you," Nika stated plainly.

Usian chuckled as he rose from his seat. Both he and Subira had been on Nika's case about using the word nigga. He really didn't mind her using the word. He just didn't want her referring to him as one. Respect was one of the things that he was going to enforce in their marriage. They would mutually respect one another, and no disrespect of any form would be tolerated.

"Bring your silly self over here," Usian said, chuckling.

Nika held her arms out to the side and stepped toward him, crossing her legs as she approached him. She looked like a belly dancer, moving toward him, and he got a kick out of the humor that Nika was displaying.

"You need to be serious, Nika," Subira said firmly. "This is not the time to act like a silly little girl!"

"Hell… she better do something to take away the fact that she's about to get her cherry popped," Jackie said, rolling her eyes. "You better have a drink or something to take the edge off, sweetie."

"It's okay, Ms. Subira," Usian assured her.

He looked at his mother disapprovingly and lifted an eyebrow. Jackie glared back at him and tilted her head to the side a bit to let his ass know *she ain't give a fuck*, and he could tell by her demeanor. "I wouldn't have it any other way, Ms. Subira. This is one of the reasons why I love Nika, and I have no problems letting her be who she is."

Subira looked at Nika and rolled her eyes. She reached down into her pocket and pulled out a handkerchief. It had some initials in the corner, and Usian wondered who they belonged to.

"Take this handkerchief, Usian, and use it for verification," Subira explained. "This belonged to my late husband, and he gave it to me specifically for this reason."

Usian took it from Subira and smirked. Next, he swung it over his head and started dancing toward Nika. Subira shook her head from side to side and laughed at the couple as they danced with one another. She knew their marriage was going to be full of laughter, joy, and love. She prayed that their marriage would be wrapped up in all of those things in order to keep their union solid.

Subira gave Nika a hug and kiss before leaving the room. Jackie did the same and gave the couple her blessing. She was about to go home and vast in the happiness of her son's marriage. Jackie wanted to invite his sister, but she promised Usian that she wouldn't tell anyone until he told her it was okay. His sister, Joyce, was married to a street nigga, so it wouldn't take much for word to get around about his marriage. Both women walked to the door and sent air kisses before leaving the newlyweds alone.

"Are you going to unwrap me or what?" Nika asked, placing her hands on her hips. "It's really hot in here, and this is why I don't agree with covering myself to appease a man."

"I don't know, wifey," Usian said, approaching her. "I think you look rather sexy."

"Ha... ha... very funny, husband," Nika replied, batting her eyes.

She was fully covered, so Usian couldn't see her facial expressions. "Did I just call you husband? I kinda like the sound of that."

Usian bent down and got on his knees, grabbing the bottom of the hijab. He looked up into Nika's eyes as he raised the covering and smiled as he continued to pull it up.

"I definitely like the sound of it," he replied, standing to his feet.

He pulled the hijab completely off and gazed at his beautiful wife. She had taken off the robe when she found out that she had to wear the hijab. Nika insisted that it would be way too hot with all of those clothes on. Plus, she wanted to look as sexy as possible for Usian. The white lace and satin nightgown were fitting her body perfectly. The top of it was made like a bustier, and the cups fit her breast perfectly. The top of it covered her nipples with the right amount of top boob and cleavage showing. Her breasts looked like plump, chocolate mounds, and it made Usian's mouth water as he stared at her. The bottom of the nightgown clung to her hips and draped all the way down to her feet. "Your mother was taking this completely covered thing serious, huh?"

Nika looked at Usian and laughed.

"What's the matter, bae? It's taking you too long to get to your kitty?"

"Yes! You're usually half naked when you come down to my apartment, so I don't have to remove so much shit," Usian complained. "Why didn't you just come naked if you were going to wear that long ass hijab?"

"That's what I said," Nika agreed. "See... great minds think alike!"

Usian took Nika into his arms and stared lovingly into her eyes before ravishing her mouth. He pressed his thick lips against Nika's and slipped his tongue deep inside. Nika moaned as she welcomed this passionate kiss and wrapped her arms around his neck. She loved the intensity of their kisses and couldn't wait to take things a step further. Usian abruptly pulled away with his brow furrowed. Nika had a confused look on her face because she didn't know what was going on.

"Did we forget something?" Usian asked, grabbing her arm.

He pulled her over toward the door and opened it wide. "I forgot to carry you over the threshold, my love."

"Ahhh… baby. That's so romantical," Nika said, gushing. "But I better get something to put in the door so that we won't get locked out of our room."

"Good idea," Usian said, leaving her standing at the door.

He walked over to the couch and grabbed one of the pillows. "This will do."

Next, he grabbed Nika by the hand and led her out of the room. He placed the pillow in between the wall and the door jam in order to keep it propped open. He swept Nika off of her feet and kissed her lips quickly. "Are you ready. Mrs. Jasper Simpson Jr?"

"I'm ready as I'll ever be, Mr. Jasper Simpson Jr."

CHAPTER

One

"I think I'm going to be sick," Nika said, running into the bathroom. "Why hasn't Usian called or messaged me?"

"You need to calm down, my child," Subira said, standing in the doorway. "I know that Usian is coming. You should have some faith in Allah."

"I do have faith in Allah, Mama," Nika assured her. "But it's Usian that I'm worried about."

Nika leaned against the bathroom sink and stared at her phone. She was trying to will it to ring, but that type of foolishness only happened in the movies. Things were perfect when she left the house this afternoon, and Usian promised that he would be at the hotel on time like they discussed. *Maybe Usian felt like too much pressure was being put on him by announcing our marriage in such a manner*, Nika thought. She never wanted to impose things on him that he didn't feel comfortable about. All she wanted to do was talk to him so that she knew that everything was okay. Nika was deep in thought when she heard the lock to the suite click. Subira turned to see who was entering the room, and a smile appeared on her face. She looked back at a nervous Nika smugly and shook her head.

"Here he is now, beloved," Subira said, moving out of the doorway.

"He's here!" Nika shouted, running out of the bathroom.

She urgently ran up to him and wrapped her arms around his neck because she was so happy to see him. However, what she did next was so unexpected.

"Where the hell were you?" Nika questioned, pushing him in the shoulder.

"Aaaahhhh... don't, Nika," Usian urged. "I'm really sore right there. I got grazed by a bullet in this shoulder."

"What! How did you get grazed?" Nika asked, looking panicked. "Who was shooting at you?"

"It's a long story, baby, and I don't want to get into it right now," Usain replied.

"I'm sorry, but you got the wrong one," Nika said, cocking her head back. "We have nothing but time, so you need to start talking, mister!"

"I'm with you, Nika," Subira second. "You need to tell us exactly what happened so that we can figure this out."

"Does this have anything to do with your extracurriculars?" Nika asked, folding her arms in front of her.

"No," Usian replied defensively. "The person that did this was trying to kidnap me!"

"Kidnap you?" Nika mocked. "Why would someone want to do some shit like that?" Nika looked over at her mother. "Sorry, Mama!"

"It's all good," Subira replied. "Because I'm wondering why someone would want to kidnap you as well. That's the most absurd thing..." Subira stopped talking and thought for a moment. Why wouldn't someone want to kidnap Usian if they felt he was a threat? Usian was the reason Nika was dragging her feet to marry Roc. Those were measures taken by a desperate man, and there were plenty of those type downstairs in the ballroom. "How many men were there, and did you get a good look at them?" Subira questioned.

"There were two men that tried to get me. The driver seemed to be the one calling all of the shots, and I didn't get a good look at him. However, the man who jumped out of the car was a big, brown-skinned guy, but I didn't get a look at his face, because it was covered with a mask," Usian explained. "I was already running late and ran out of the lounge so that I could go home and shower."

"You shouldn't have been at the lounge in the first place!" Nika fussed. "You knew you had to be here so that we could taaaalk!"

Nika bucked her eyes at him because they had agreed to have a quickie before they went down to the celebration. "But you had to carr' yo' ass down there to see Whisper! Is this how our marriage is going to be? You always running your ass down to the lounge to hang with Whisper?"

"This is not the time to throw a temper tantrum, baby," Usian advised. "A nigga tried to take me against my will, and I don't know who the hell it was! The nigga even hit me in the head with his gun."

"What!" Nika shouted. "And what did you do?"

"I didn't do shi—" Usian looked at Subira.

"Go ahead, Usian. It's okay," Subira assured him.

"I didn't do shit, because I was in pain," Usian said, aggravated. "He tried to make me get in the car, but I refused. There was no way I was just going to voluntarily go to my death."

"How did you get out of it?" Nika asked, cuddling up to his good side.

"It was all Big Lee and her girls," Usian explained. "Ew Baby had seen what was happening when she looked out of the kitchen window at her mother's house. She called out to Big Lee and Lay to get the guns, and they came out of Big Lee's house, shooting like they were in the wild west; they had some big shit too! They tore a new frame out of the car those dudes were in, and when the driver told ole boy to come on, he fired a shot off at me. I fell backward as he jumped into the car and sped off. I'm telling you, baby, I was almost a dead man, and that's what had happened."

"I'm willing to bet money that Roc had something to do with this nonsense," Nika said, frowning. "His dumb butt loves to watch all of those kidnapping movies that be on Netflix and *Lifetime*. I'm sure his dumb ass best friend was in on it too."

"I promise you, Allah as my witness, if I find out he had anything to do with this, I'm killing him," Usian promised. "It was obvious that whoever is behind this wanted me to be gone. Why wouldn't he want the man who has stolen his future wife to disappear?"

"I wonder if his father or Jumba put him up to doing this?" Nika uttered. "They're not beyond doing something so foolish... are they?"

"If Jumba was behind something like this, he wouldn't do a kidnapping. He would merely pay someone to kill Usian and make sure it didn't get traced back to him," Subira replied frankly.

"I don't think your uncle has anything to do with this," Usian assured Nika. "This was some amateur hour type stuff. The nigga who tried to grab me and the driver's voice sounded familiar. I can't put my finger on it, but I'm sure it will come to me."

"I'm just glad that you're okay," Nika said, pressing her forehead against his. "I don't know what I would have done if anything had happened to you." She kissed his lips tenderly.

"Nothing was going to keep me from you," Usain said, half smiling. "I love you, wife of mine."

"And I love you, husband of mine."

They kissed again but this time let it linger for a few minutes. Subira walked away from them and went over to stare out of the window. She was furious that someone would try such a thing, and on the last day of Ramadan! She would get to the bottom of this if it was the last thing she did in life.

Everyone had started feasting on the wonderful spread of meats, vegetables, fruits, cakes, and other fare that Meme had provided. People were seated at various tables around the room, and the banter was filling the space. Several hours had already passed, and Subira nor Nika had yet to make an appearance. There was so much tension in the room that it could be cut with a knife, and Meme was getting a kick out of all of it. Usia had come to her and asked if she'd talked to Subira, and Meme assured her that their sister would be in attendance. Usia tried to small talk her and ask questions about Nika as well, but Meme sidestepped her inquiries and excused herself from the conversation. Meme had some strong feelings toward her big sister, and she didn't appreciate what Jumba was trying to pull with Nika's arranged marriage. Soon, she, Nika, and Subira would have the last laugh, and Meme would throw all of it up in their smug faces every chance that she got.

Subira walked into the ballroom in a lovely orange and gold African print dress with the matching hijab. The bold gold and sapphire jewelry that she wore complimented her smooth, ebony skin, along with the bright fabrics that adorned her body. She spoke and exchanged pleasantries with people as she made her way over to the table where her now sworn enemies were seated. She had an announcement to make to all of them, and she wanted to make sure they got a good view of her when she spoke.

"Look who finally decided to show up," Jumba said arrogantly. "We've been waiting on you and your daughter all night. Where is Nika?"

"She's with her husband, and good evening to you too," Subira replied smugly.

"Excuse me... What did you just say?" Baraka asked, looking puzzled.

"Oh, you heard me correct," Subira replied nonchalantly. "Amanika will not be joining us tonight, because someone tried to abduct her husband, Usian. We had planned this grand entrance to announce their union, but one of you worthless pigs tried to have him kidnapped."

"What! That's absurd!" Jumba shouted. "What do you mean, Nika is married to Usian? More importantly... why are you trying to say that any of us had anything to do with someone trying to kidnap Usian?" Baraka added.

Roc had gone out to take a smoke break and noticed Subira standing at the table with his parents and godparents. He hightailed it over to their table because he wanted to know where his future bride was hiding. He tried to call Pooh to see if he successfully grabbed Usian, but his phone kept going straight to voicemail. Roc assumed that everything went well because no news was better than good news. However, he had a feeling that something was wrong.

"Hey, Subira," Roc said, walking up from behind. "Where is Nika?"

Subira turned and glared at Roc like he had shit on his face. She really didn't like Roc as a person nor as a husband for her daughter. She paid attention to the way he spoke and treated Nika, and here and now, lately, Roc had been very disrespectful. Subira saw the way he would grab Nika and speak to her disrespectfully. She couldn't wait for the day that Usian beat his ass, and hopefully, it was coming sooner than later. "Is she here with you?" Roc asked, looking around.

"My daughter is with her husband, and I came here to inform you all that this fiasco is over. Nika and Usian got married a few days before Ramadan and have been married for a month now," Subira announced happily. "It was a small wedding at the mosque, and only real family members and close friends were invited."

"This is ridiculous!" Baraka shouted, slamming his fist on the table.

"You have to be joking, right?" Roc asked, looking around the room. "Where are the cameras? It's obvious we're being punked!"

"You were punked when you thought I was going to let you marry my daughter!" Subira shot back. "Your father is a sworn enemy of my husband's, and did you think for an inkling of a minute that I would let my most prized possession marry into your family?"

"You are such a foolish old bitch!" Jumba seethed. "You couldn't let the shit go, could you?"

"Jumba!" Usia called out in outrage. "That's my sister!"

Jumba looked over at her in disgust. "I don't give a fuck!" Jumba shouted. "She owes us half a million dollars, and I want my money!"

"I don't owe you a got damn thing, you ignorant piece of shit!" Subira yelled! "If anything, you owe me, you old pompous asshole! I've done my fair share of helping you and your pathetic wife out!"

"Subira... why are you saying these things?" Usia questioned sadly. "You're my sister, and I love you!"

"You don't love me, Usia, because if you did, then you wouldn't have agreed to or pushed the issue of Nika marrying Roc. You knew as well as anyone that my husband hated Baraka and tried to kill him numerous times back home! You were just as much a part of this debauchery as those two, and I will never forgive you for it!"

"I must say that I'm flabbergasted," Adisa said, clutching her pearls. "Nika's no prize, if I might say so myself, and if you would have raised her properly, she would have conformed and married Roc straight out of high school like we planned."

Subira turned to face Adisa because she really had a problem with her. She didn't like the way Adisa was always trying to attack Nika because she didn't follow the requirements of their faith. Adisa was a brainwashed idiot that followed whatever her husband told her to do. She was the type of woman that Subira didn't want Nika to turn out to be, and if she would have married Roc, this would have eventually been Nika's fate.

"You need to shut the fuck up and remain quiet like normal," Meme said, approaching the table. "My niece is a prize, and that's why all you greedy muthafuckas are trying to get your hands on her!"

"She's just as ignorant at Subira!" Jumba fussed. "I can't believe all of my hard work is gone down the drain! I hope you're happy, you old, miserable bitch!"

"Actually, I'm very happy," Subira replied, smiling. "Just to see the look on all of your miserable ass faces has made my year! I prayed all day and night during the holy month of Ramadan and asked Allah to clear the path. Allah is the best knower, and it was destined for Nika to marry Usian."

"I bet she's pregnant! That's why they hurried off to be married!" Jumba shouted. "Subira knew that Nika wasn't a virgin, so she tried to hurry up and marry her off in order to not make herself look bad!"

Subira reached into her purse and pulled out a blood-stained handkerchief. She held it up in the air proudly as she threw her head and shoulders back. There was no way she was going to let them slander her daughter's virtue.

"You wish that was the reason why my daughter married Usian," Subira replied arrogantly. "This blood-stained handkerchief was given to me by my son-in-law after he took my daughter's virginity. Usian walked it down to my room and gave it to me in front of several witnesses, including my sister Meme and her husband. It would have been so convenient for you to tell that lie to everyone after they discovered that none of you worthless pieces of trash got a dime from me!"

"That is enough!" Baraka demanded. "You have managed to make a mockery out of this entire situation, Subira, and you and your daughter will pay for it! I will sue the both of you for everything that you got and won't rest until you're homeless and living out of a box!"

"My money is long, nigga, so do what you gotta do," Subira replied smugly. "I can buy your worthless ass three times and still be able to live my best life!"

"That's a good one," Meme whispered to Subira.

Subira looked over at her sister and winked.

"Where the fuck is Nika!" Roc demanded.

"I told you she's with her husband," Subira replied. "And if I find out that you were the one behind the attempted kidnapping of my son-in-law. I'm going to make sure that he beats you to a bloody pulp, and your family will not be able to recognize you!"

"Your idle threats mean nothing," Roc replied, laughing. "I'm not afraid of you. And I'm definitely not afraid of Usian!"

"You better be," Subira warned. "Because he's coming to get you!"

CHAPTER

"We should have gone downstairs," Usian complained. "You see I have my riders with me, so shit would have been handled if need be."

"Definitely," Whisper replied. "Whoever sent those niggas were must not have known the force behind Usian. They were very disrespectful, sending them to grab my dude while he was on the set. It's obvious they don't know about a real Ville nigga! We about to shut shit down!"

"All that's not necessary," Nika said, sitting down next to Usian on the couch. "I'm sure Roc's dumb ass is behind this shit, and he's really harmless, but he has a best friend that's a drug dealer. He hangs out a bunch of random lounges, and I've seen him talking to some real gangsta ass niggas."

"How do you know what gangsta niggas look like?" CJ asked, chuckling.

Nika glared over at CJ with a scowl on her face. She didn't appreciate him making the assumption that she didn't know what a street nigga looked like. Nika lived in the hood and grew up the majority of her life over on Cora where they currently lived. She went to a St. Louis Public School like everyone else and graduated. Nika had witnessed a variety of violent acts. Drive-by shootings were frequent, especially walking home from school. She graduated from Sumner High School, so leaving school at the end of the day was always a gamble. The school was located in a Crip neighborhood, and dudes from all different sets went to school there.

Luckily, Subira picked Nika up as many days as she could because Nika and Kimmie hated walking down Billups Avenue to Cote Brilliant Avenue.

"You got my baby fucked up!" Usian hissed defensively. "My wife grew up on Cora, nigga, so she knows what's up. Yo' stupid ass is the one who ain't hip, and some shit is about to change from here on out. I have a wife now, and it's time for me to change up my life. I'm not going to be in these streets for too much longer, because I'm working on building my family."

Usian put his hand on Nika's knee and squeezed it before placing a kiss on her lips. Nika touched the side of his face endearingly and smiled as she gazed into his eyes.

"Well said, lover," Nika uttered, turning her attention toward CJ. "CJ, I hang out in lounges with some of the most gutter niggas in the Lou. I be in the Gateway, and I'm married to a gangsta, so why wouldn't I be able to spot one?"

"Geesh... I'm sorry," CJ apologized. "I didn't mean to step on anyone's toes."

Everyone started laughing at him.

"It's all good, lil' nigga! Just watch yo' mouth when you making assumptions about my baby!" Usian said, standing. "Since we're not going downstairs to the party, let's pop this bottle and toast to me and my wife and the end of Ramadan! May Allah grant us a prosperous year!"

Everyone piled into the elevator so they could head to their cars and go to the Gateway Lounge. They were about to go celebrate the union of Usian and Nika Ville style since they weren't able to kick it after the wedding. Ramadan started the next day, and Subira was insistent on making sure that Usian and Nika were focused on repenting all of their sins and praying to Allah for prosperity and longevity in their marriage. Nika texted Subira to let her know that they had left the hotel. Subira decided to stay at the celebration because she was getting a kick out of making everyone uncomfortable. She sat at the same table as Jumba, Usia, Baraka, and Adisa on purpose. Her two sisters, Zaida and Meme, sat next to Subira in solidarity while the haters on the other side threw daggers with their eyes. What added insult to injury was the people coming up to

Subira, asking questions and offering their congratulations to Nika on her marriage.

The elevator door opened, and everyone filed out in good spirits. They were laughing and joking with one another as they headed toward the front door. Usian was leading the pack with Nika in tow. They were holding hands and walking lazily when Usian stopped to kiss his wife. He spun her around and dipped her while their friends made comments. Kimmie, Mac, Whisper, and CJ were cracking jokes, but the couple didn't care as they kissed each other passionately. Usian brought her back up to her feet and kissed her lips quickly once more.

"What the fuck is all of this!" Roc yelled angrily. "And what the fuck is this I hear about the two of you being married?"

Everyone looked around to see who was making the statement. Roc walked up to Usian and Nika with a few men with him. He was at the highest point of being pissed off and was ready to get to the bottom of the bullshit. "Bitch! You're promised to me, and there's no way you're going to get out of the agreement that our families—"

"You got me fucked up!" Usian spat.

Bam! Usian punched Roc square in the nose, causing him to fall backward onto the floor.

"Daaaaaayyyyyuuuuummmmm!" CJ shouted.

Usian was still holding Nika's hand and let it go before he charged over to Roc. A couple of the men who were with Roc tried to stop Usian, but Whisper lifted his shirt and shook his head. Usian pushed past the men, bumping one of them so hard that he stumbled over to the side. Usian walked up on Roc, bending down with an evil grimace on his face. He open-hand slapped Roc in the face and pointed his finger, pushing Roc in the head while chastising him.

"Don't you ever fix your lips to disrespect my muthafuckin wife again! Nigga, I'll kill you about that one, and yo' bitch ass better address *my wife* as Mrs. Simpson, hoe ass nigga!"

"What's going on?" Baraka asked, running up to Usian. "Who the hell are you!"

"This is the degenerate that Subira claims is married to Nika," Jumba said, breathing heavily.

He and Baraka ran out to the lobby when one of the men that was with

Roc came and told them that Roc was getting jumped by some men. "This is Usian!"

"Young man, why are you attacking my son?" Baraka inquired angrily. "He's down on the ground, and any respectable man would give him time to get up off the ground."

"I don't respect bitch ass niggas who disrespect my wife," Usian retorted aggressively.

"You don't owe them any explanation," Nika said, grabbing Usian by the arm. "Come on, and let's go."

"Wait a minute, Nika," Jumba said, trying to grab her by the arm.

Usian took her by the arm and pushed her behind him forcefully. Next, he stood straight up and stared Jumba directly in his eyes with a calm expression on his. He wasn't trying to whoop anyone else's ass, but he would happily oblige whomever.

"You will not touch her," Usian said sternly. "If you have something to say to her, then say it to me."

"You can't speak to me like that! I'm her uncle, her father's brother, and I'm the overseer of their family!" Jumba yelled. "I don't know what nonsense Subira and Nika have filled your head with, but Nika is promised to Roc! We have papers to support the agreement made with Abdalla, Nika's father, and I intend on following through with my brother's wishes, even if it kills me doing it!"

"That can be arranged," CJ said, walking up next to Usian.

Usian looked over at CJ and nodded his head. He held up his finger to silence his nephew because making threats like that while a bunch of witnesses were around wasn't wise. He was still teaching his nephew, but CJ was going to have to grow up fast because Usian realized all shit was about to pop off.

"You don't oversee shit except that bitch of a wife of yours and those ungrateful ass brats you call kids!" Nika yelled, outraged. "You're no kin to me, faker… imposter! You were going to sell me to your own brother's enemy; you're a disgraceful asshole!"

Nika was leaning to the side because Usian wouldn't let her pass him when she tried to walk toward Jumba. She tooted her lips up and spat at Jumba because she hated him with a passion. He was a money grubber that didn't deserve a dime, and if Nika had her way, Jumba would be dead.

Roc had gotten up off the ground, but his nose was bleeding profusely. His father had given him a handkerchief, but it was quickly saturated with blood.

"I think my nose is broken!" Roc cried out in pain.

"Be happy that I was holding Nika's hand because if I would have brought the force behind it, your ass would be knocked the fuck out!" Usian uttered arrogantly. "And like I said, you better watch how you talk to my wife!"

"What is this wife nonsense that you all keep talking about?" Baraka asked intently. "I know that Subira came to the table, uttering some foolishness and waving a stained handkerchief, but that doesn't mean anything, not unless I see a marriage license."

"We have one of those, but we don't have to show you shit," Nika replied, peeking from behind Usian. "Allah knows what's up!"

"Are you using the Lord's name in vain?" Baraka asked angrily. "You will produce a legal document stating that you are married to this man, Nika, or else we will proceed with the arrangements that are being made for your *real marriage*!"

"This is a real marriage, bitch ass nigga!" Usian insisted in an aggravated tone. "I'm tired of standing here. Let's go, Nika, before I hurt one of these niggas for real!"

"Don't think that this is the end!" Roc called out. "You have made a huge mistake!"

"Like you did sending them niggas to try to kidnap me," Usian replied, lifting an eyebrow. "Next time, find some professionals because those amateurs were way out of their league."

Usian chuckled and turned to leave. He grabbed a handful of Nika's ass and kissed her passionately. Roc, Jumba, and Baraka looked on angrily as Usian made a spectacle of the entire situation. Usian didn't give a fuck about any of those dudes, and he was ready for anybody that wanted to run the fuck up.

CHAPTER

Three

$\mathcal{U}$ sian and Nika went down to the Gateway to party with their friends. Nika called Subira and told her about what happened in the lobby on their car ride to the lounge. Subira laughed with satisfaction as Nika laughed and told the story. She was very animated, and Usian got a kick out of listening to her. Subira said that she heard the young man when he came to tell Jumba and Baraka what was going on. Subira said that Usia and Adisa wanted to go out there as well, but their husbands insisted that they stay in the ballroom. Subira stated that she wanted to punch both of the women sitting across from her in the face. However, the smile she wore on her face was more damaging and said a lot.

Drinks had been flowing for over two hours, and the happy couple was having the time of their life. People were coming up to them, giving their congratulations, and Mac was telling stories about when he and Usian were kids. Big Lee had called and had a cake made on short notice to present to the couple. Sam's always had a cake ready to purchase, and they didn't need a big one anyway. Mac had popped four bottles of champagne, and Whisper was about to take over and pop even more. Usian was standing over by the bar, talking with his friends, while Nika was sitting at the table, talking with Kimmie, Big Lee, and Lay, Big Lee's daughter.

He looked over and smiled when her face lit up in laughter. She was the most beautiful woman that he'd ever seen, and he wanted to dance with his wife. She was wearing a long, white dress that fit her breasts snugly then flowed down to her feet. She had gotten her hair straightened, and it draped down to the middle of her back, and the gold and diamond tiara she wore on top of her head was fitting. She looked like an angel in Usian's eyes—his angel—and he was going to protect her with his life.

He went over to the DJ's booth and asked him to play the song he played when he made love to his wife for the first time. He walked over to Nika and bent over, kissing her lips softly as the song came on. He grabbed her by the hand and pulled her on the dance floor while everyone cat-called after them. Nika was embarrassed and blushed the entire time they walked over to the dancefloor, not because of the people making comments but from the song that was playing. It had a symbolic meaning for them, and only the two of them knew what it represented. Usian twirled her around in a circle before drawing her close. He kissed her lips tenderly as they began to sway their bodies to the music.

THEIR WEDDING NIGHT...

I think I must be dreaming that you are here with me. Must have died and gone to heaven, and it's all that I hoped it would be...

Nika was nervously standing in front of Usian in the beautiful gown that her mother had bought. They were about to consummate their marriage, and Nika was nervous as hell. Usian had put on "Still in Love" by Brian McKnight from a playlist he had made to commemorate this moment. He put all the songs that reminded him of Nika and how she made him feel on this list and planned on making love to her all night to it. Usian swept her up in his arms and carried her into the bedroom.

She planted soft kisses over his face and kissed him tenderly once they made it to the bed. He lowered her on top of it and used his weight to push Nika on her back. He hovered over her with a smirk on his face before he stood up and grabbed her by the ankle. He reached into his pocket and threw the handkerchief that Subira gave him on one of the pillows. Next, he pulled her butt to the edge of the bed, kissing the back of her calf. Nika giggled at the tickling sensation that it was giving her, and Usian found it amusing. He let it go and grabbed the hem of her gown, trying to lift it up, but Nika grabbed his hands.

"Wait... stop!" Nika shouted, sitting up. "Uhhh... you are my husband, and I should be the one pleasing you."

Nika pushed Usian back and climbed out of the bed. "I have something planned, and I think you're going to like it."

Usian looked at Nika curiously and figured he would humor her. It wasn't like they had anywhere to go, and he had all night to break that tight little snatch open.

"What is this about, woman?" Usian joked. "I am ready to get up in those guts, and yo' ass is bullshitting."

"I'm not bullshitting," Nika insisted. "I think that it should be ladies first since my virginity is worth so much money. I'm supposed to be a gift to you, so let me show you that I was worth the wait."

"If that makes you happy, then I'm all for it," Usian said, smiling. "What do you want me to do?"

Nika looked around the room for a second, trying to remember what she and Kimmie had planned. Her nerves were getting to her, and she thought the vape and champagne would help ease her anxiety. However, she could hear and feel her heart beat in her ears, and that made things worse.

"Can you go grab that chair over there and bring it over here," Nika instructed.

She was standing in front of the bed and felt this would be the best place to start. Usian did as she asked and brought the chair over to her. He set it down and chuckled because he had an idea of what was about to happen. "Sit down while I get something," Nika said, walking away from him. Usian did as he was told and sat down on the chair. He took off the silk pajama top that he was wearing and threw it on the floor. Nika walked back over to him with a cup of ice and a pillow.

"What you about to do with that?" Usian questioned, lifting an eyebrow.

"I'm about to do what you wouldn't let me do before we got married," Nika replied smugly. "Do you have a problem with it?"

"Naw... I ain't got a problem with it. I was merely asking a question."

"Well, don't ask no questions. Just sit there and enjoy what I'm about to do to you."

"Yes, ma'am," Usian replied, smiling.

He liked how aggressive Nika was being, and this was the appropriate time that her ass needed to talk slick to him. It wouldn't be tolerated outside the bedroom, and Usian would teach his young wife this as they continued to learn about one another.

Nika placed the pillow down on the floor in front of Usian and took a step back. She pulled her nightgown over her head, exposing another secret underneath it. Usian stared in shock because he wasn't sure what he was looking at. Nika giggled a little at Usian's response. She knew that this moment would be amusing, and she was enjoying every second of it.

"What the fuck is that?" Usian asked, perplexed.

"This is a chastity belt that I would have had to wear if I were back in Africa with my father. He asked my mother to make me wear this, but she didn't want to. Mama felt that in this day in age, to make me wear it was ridiculous. Besides, we were in America, and people don't really do this anymore. My father was old school and apparently quite crazy," Nika explained, laughing.

"How do I get you out of that thing?" Usian probed.

The chastity belt was made of gold and silk. It was made in the shape of a pair of thongs and had three thick, gold bars that wrapped around each side of her waist and came from the back in between her legs and up to her waist. The crotch part was lined in silk so that it didn't irritate Nika, but it felt uncomfortable all the same. They were all connected into a lock that sat in the middle of her pelvis. "Is that a lock that needs a key?" Usian asked, inspecting the contraption.

"You should already have the key. My mother gave it to you... Remember?"

Usian thought about it for a minute and snapped his finger. He reached into his pocket and pulled out a gold key tied to a piece of silk. Subira told him that this was the key to his happiness when she gave it to him, and Usian didn't understand what she meant until this very moment.

"I do have the key!" Usian announced happily.

"Good! Now can you take this shit off of me? It is terribly uncomfortable, and I can't perform my wifely duties with this shit on," Nika fussed.

Usian looked on and laughed as she complained. He wanted her to leave it on because it was sexy as fuck, almost primitive in a sense, but he knew Nika wasn't going to go for it. "C'mon and unlock this muthafucka, nigga!"

Usian glared at her.

"What did I tell you about calling me that shit?" Usian roared. Get down on your knees, and assume the fucking position!"

Nika's eyes bucked open in fear, and she dropped to her knees instantly. Usian didn't look intimidating, but she was nervous all the same. Nika knew that she had surrendered herself to Usian when they got married, and she had to do what was asked of her by him. "Please understand that you will talk to me with the utmost respect. Now, I don't give a fuck about you talking shit to me, but you will do it respectfully, and calling me that word is not permitted. Do I make myself clear?"

"Yes," Nika uttered softly. "Don't call you a nigga."

"Exactly."

"Okay. Now take this shit off of me... husband," Nika shot back. "You know you got me fucked up, don't you? But I won't disrespect you by calling you a nigga."

Usian laughed before he leaned down and kissed her lips. He loved her smart-mouthed ass and was ready to have his way with her. He grabbed her by the back of her head and pulled her up to her feet. He stuck the key inside and unlocked the belt. They both looked at each other when it made a clicking sound before coming unfastened. "Boy! My mama and daddy were on some bullshit!"

"I kind of like this contraption. I might put your ass in it when I leave the house in the morning to make sure you don't give my pussy away," Usian joked.

"They have them for men too, you know. My mama has one in her closet, and I bet it will fit," Nika replied, smugly. "You're the one with the lingering dick."

"The only place this dick is going to linger is inside of you," Usian replied sarcastically.

Usian helped Nika take the belt off and threw it over to the side. Nika got back down on her knees in front of Usian and looked up at him, biting her bottom lip. Her eyes brightened when she reached inside of his pajama pants and pulled out his long, thick dick. She had never held one in her hand, but she touched one in middle school on a dare. Nika was surprised at how soft it felt because, for some reason, she thought it would be clammy.

"Are going to sit there and stare at it, or are you going to put this cold muthafucka in yo' mouth?"

"I..." Nika said, gulping. "I'm going to put it in my mouth."

She put her hand around the girth of his joint and pressed the tip to her lips. She licked the precum that was sitting at the opening and frowned up her face. She pulled it away and looked up at Usian in disgust.

"It's salty," Nika mumbled, drawing up her face.

"Just put it in your mouth, and I'll help you do the rest," Usian offered.

"I don't need you to help me!" Nika snapped. "I know what I'm doing... I think."

Nika opened her mouth and placed Usian's rod in her mouth. It was semi-hard, so she didn't feel that intimidated. She sucked her jaws in and pulled it in and out like Kimmie instructed. She gagged as it grew in her mouth, and pulled out, coughing profusely.

"Ahhh... this muthafucka gets bigger," Usian warned her.

"I see," Nika replied, still coughing.

"Do it again, but take your time. Don't try to take the whole thing in your mouth. Take it in a little at a time," Usian advised. "That bitch Kimmie is a pro at sucking dick, and using a popsicle ain't quite the same."

Usian remembered the day Kimmie called herself teaching Nika how to suck dick with a popsicle. His manhood thumped as he thought about it, and Nika looked at it strangely. She put the head into her mouth again and slowly worked the tip. Usian bit down on his bottom lip as he watched Nika intently. She was building up her confidence slowly, taking more and more into her mouth. She would gag periodically but continued to work him in her mouth.

Usian put his hand behind her head and controlled her pace to make sure she wouldn't kill herself. He could easily choke her if he pushed all of his length down her throat. The slob was building up in her mouth, and Nika didn't seem like she was coming up anytime soon. She reached down and started fondling his balls roughly, and Usian grabbed her hand. He took it and placed it on his chest. They would have to work on that, but right now, he needed her to master the art of sucking dick.

Nika pulled it out of her mouth and spat on it. She moved her hand back and forth, jacking it while staring at him lustfully. She reached down and put a piece of ice in her mouth and sucked on it for a few seconds. Her jaws were hurting, and it didn't look like Usian was going to nut anytime soon. She placed the tip of his rod back in her mouth and rubbed the ice against the shaft. Usian held his head back and let out a long sigh as she continued to work him in her mouth. He slowly humped her face and guided her through her first dick suck, but he was ready to run up inside of his wife's tight honey pot.

"Come here," Usian said, lifting her up. "I want some of this good stuff."

He reached down in between her legs and felt her wetness on his fingers. He brought them up to his mouth and licked her juices off his fingers. "Damn, baby. Sucking my dick made you wet like this?"

Nika giggled while Usian put his fingers back in between her legs and played with her nub. He rubbed his knuckle against it while Nika rocked her pelvis against it. Usian reached his free hand up and put it around Nika's neck. He pulled her face down toward him and kissed her lips passionately. They slipped their tongues into each other's mouths and kissed nastily while Usian played with his kitty. He took one of Nika's nipples into his mouth, and she moaned when he bit down on it. He sucked hard and flickered his tongue against it, making Nika shake. He wanted her to cum before inserting himself inside of her because he wanted to make sure she was well lubricated. He knew it was going to hurt her, so he wanted to make it as comfortable as possible.

"I'm about to cum, bae," Nika moaned. "Uuuuhhhh…"

Nika came all over Usian's hand, and he smiled with satisfaction. She was right where he wanted her, and now it was time for him to get his prize. He was about to pop Nika's cherry and consummate their marriage finally.

"Climb on top of my lap," Usian instructed.

"Okay," Nika replied nervously.

"It's okay, baby," Usian said, kissing her lips. "I'm going to be gentle with you. Do you trust me?"

"Yes," Nika whispered, climbing on his lap. "I trust you with my life."

They stared into each other's eyes intensely while Usian rubbed the tip of his erection against her wet folds. Nika licked his lips before pressing hers against his. They kissed nastily, and Nika sucked in air when she felt a bit of pressure in between her legs.

"Relax," Usian said against her lips. "I want you to take some deep breaths. It's not going to feel good going in, but I'm going to be as gentle as I can."

"Ooooo… kay…" Nika whined.

Usian pushed up into Nika a bit more, and her head fell on his shoulder. It was hurting, and a part of her wanted to stop. Usian pushed in a little more, and this time, Nika cried out in pain.

"Wait a minute," Nika cried out. "I don't know if I'm ready for this! It hurts, bae… It hurts!"

"Ssshhh… ssshhh…" Usian cooed. "I know it hurts right now, baby, but it's going to feel good once I get you opened up. Look at me, Nika."

At first, Nika kept her face buried in his shoulder, but he repeated his command again firmly, and she held her head up. She stared into his eyes, and he planted a soft kiss on her lips. He kissed her shoulder then her breast before he took her nipple in his mouth. He bit down real hard on it and pushed himself all the way inside of Nika. Surges of pain shot through Nika, and she didn't know which one to respond too. Usian swirled his tongue around her nipple and suckled it gently. There was a bit of a burning sensation in between Nika's legs, and she wasn't aware of what to do.

"I'm inside, baby," Usian mentioned, kissing her shoulder softly. "I want you to relax and let me do all of the work. Okay?"

"O… kay," Nika uttered painfully.

Her face was balled up, and Usian could tell she was uncomfortable. He placed his hands on both of her hips and slowly worked her up and down on his stiff erection. Nika whined and moaned as he continued to work himself inside of her. Her walls felt so tight that Usian found it hard to get a tempo going. He closed his eyes and bit his bottom lip as she gripped him with each stroke. Usian tried to control himself, but he could no longer take it. He needed to gain full control of this situation, and this position wasn't getting it.

He picked Nika up, and she wrapped her legs around his waist. He used one of his hands to push his pants down his legs and stepped out of them before he headed toward the bed. He went and laid them down on top of it without taking himself out of her. Nika continued to whine as he slowly worked himself inside of her. He spread her legs wider with his hands and pushed in and out, speeding up his pace. Nika was wet as hell, and she felt so damn good. Usian couldn't help himself and went to work on his wife.

He sped up his pace and devoured her insides while she cried out in pain. He pressed his lips against hers and intertwined his fingers with hers. He pumped harder and harder, faster and faster until he erupted inside of her. Usian collapsed on top of her while breathing heavily. This felt like a power nut he was releasing, and Usian couldn't remember when he nutted so hard before. He rose up and looked down into Nika's eyes, feeling overwhelmed with love and devotion. He kissed her lips quickly and wiped the sweat off her brow.

"Are you alright, baby?" he asked lovingly.

"Yes, I'm fine," Nika replied quietly. "This did not feel good like everyone said it would. Well, Kimmie and Mama said it would hurt the first few times, but I feel like my insides are going to fall out."

"That's because this was your first time. It's going to hurt the next few times we do it as well because your uterus has to get used to this big muthafucka going up in it," Usian explained.

Usian kissed her lips again and grabbed her around the neck. He squeezed tightly and looked at her with a crazed look in his eyes. "I will kill you if you ever give my pussy away to another nigga! I'm not playing with you, Amanika!"

"Boy, please," Nika said dismissively. "Quit playing!"

Usian increased the pressure of his hand around her neck, and his brow furrowed.

"I'm not playing with your ass, Amanika. If you ever fuck another man, I'm going to kill him and make you watch before I kill you," Usian replied sternly. The crazy way Usian was staring at her, she knew he meant business. "Do I make myself clear?"

"Perfectly," Nika uttered. "You ain't about to be all possessive and shit, are you?"

"It all depends on you," he replied sternly. "It all depends on you."

Nika looked into his eyes and smiled warmly. She loved Usian with everything she had inside of her, and no man would ever be able to take his place. Nika wouldn't even think of entertaining the thought of another man, because she was married to the greatest man in the whole entire world.

"I love you forever and always, Usian, and I will never have eyes for another man," Nika assured him.

"That's what I want to hear," Usian replied, smiling. "I love you too, infinitely, and I promise to love, honor, and cherish you for the rest of my life."

He leaned down and kissed her lips passionately, pulling himself out of her. Nika winced and pulled away from their kiss. Usian looked down at his limp member and saw the blood on it. A satisfying smile appeared on his face. He reached up on the pillow and grabbed the handkerchief that Subira gave him. This was the evidence that Subira wanted, and Usian wanted to make sure he honored her wishes. He loved Subira infinitely as well and was happy that they were now a family.

Usian got off the elevator two floors down from their suite. He was on his way to see Subira to give her the proof that she'd asked for. He drew a bath and put Nika in it to soak while he went to handle their first order of business as a married couple. He promised her another round when he got back, but he wanted them to take a bath and relax before they tried again. He came so hard and long inside of her that he knew it wouldn't be long before Nika got pregnant.

Usian made it to Subira's door and knocked on it firmly. He stepped back so that she could see him through the peephole, and smiled when she opened the door.

"Ahhh… Usian," Subira said, smiling. "I take it everything went well, the way you're smiling at me."

Usian held up the blood-stained handkerchief and continued to smile brightly.

"Here is the evidence you asked for," Usian said, handing her the handkerchief.

Tears welled up in Subira's eyes as she took it out of his hand. He grabbed him and hugged him tightly because they were telling her the truth. She wasn't sure to believe Nika and Usian because they had been so secretive before. She should have known that neither one of them would lie to her, but for that, she asked Allah to forgive her.

"Where is Nika? Is she alright?" Subira asked, concerned.

"Nika is fine," Usian assured her. "I left her upstairs in a hot bath, and now that I have brought you what you required, I'm about to go back upstairs and join her. You have a good night, Ms. Subira."

"It's Mama now, son," Subira replied proudly.

Usian looked at her and smiled warmly. He grabbed her free hand and kissed it softly.

"And I am honored to call you that."

A Week Later...

Roc had finished his shift at the hospital and was headed out the door when Jumba stopped him. He wasn't sure what he wanted, but hopefully, it was some good news. Everyone was walking around stressed out over the situation, and no one was as devastated as Jumba. He needed that money that was promised to him, and he didn't know how he was going to pay his creditors all of the money that he owed.

"Did you talk to your father?" Jumba asked sternly.

"No, sir. Is there a problem? Were you able to get any more information about Nika?" Roc probed.

"I haven't talked to Subira, but according to both of my wife's other sisters, the marriage is legal. They were at the ceremony and saw the minister sign their marriage certificate. I'm consulting my lawyer to see if I have grounds to sue them."

"My father is looking into the same thing. He said he'd ask one of the other lawyers at the law firm. I guess great minds think alike," Roc replied.

"That is true, and we're both wondering how you fucked this up. You had been dating Nika for a very long time. How is it that another man was able to push up on her?" Jumba questioned. "You should have had that shit on lock, and the last thing Nika should have been doing is looking in another man's direction!"

"It's not my fault! Usian lived up under Nika and her mother. I believe he got to Nika through Subira, and that's how they got together. He was always brown nosing with Subira, and for a moment I thought him and her had something going on," Roc explained. "You knew as well as anyone that Subira hated my father. Why wouldn't she want our marriage to fail? Nika's father and my father were sworn enemies."

"This is true, but you should have solidified your bond. Did you try to fuck her or suck her up at least while you were together?"

Roc looked at Jumba in shock.

"She was a virgin, and I was waiting for us to be married before I tried to have sex with her," Roc replied, outraged.

He was lying to Jumba and had tried to screw her several times, but Nika wasn't having it. Nika wouldn't even kiss him on the lips, let alone let him touch her. Roc was over this conversation and wanted to get as far away from his godfather as possible. Roc's phone started ringing, and that was his way out of this conversation. He reached down into his pocket and grabbed his phone. He looked at the screen and held his finger up.

"I really need to take this call. I'll talk to you later, Jumba," Roc assured him. "Hello."

Roc walked away from Jumba as fast as he could. Jumba had wasted enough of his time, accusing him of shit. He had plans on getting the bitch Nika back by hurting Usian. "I hope you got some good news for me."

"It depends on what you consider good news. I've located Pooh, but he's not doing so well. He got shot in the shoulder when they attempted to snatch Usian. He's laid up over on the east side and won't be back in St. Louis for a while," Carlos explained.

"I thought you said that nigga knew what he was doing!" Roc yelled, opening the door to his car.

His voice echoed in the parking garage, but luckily, no one was around. Roc hadn't heard from Pooh to find out what happened. It was obvious that Usian wasn't jammed up, because he punched the shit out of Roc in the hotel lobby. He was lucky that Usian didn't break his nose. He merely busted a few blood vessels, and Roc had recovered in a few weeks. "I have a sprained nose because of this bitch ass nigga; not to mention, I won't be getting any of the money I need to pay for school. My father's going to flip his fucking lid when he finds out that I spent my tuition on something other than school!"

"Look, Roc, I'm working on getting the money to pay for school. I was able to work out something to replace the dope. It's not my fault that it's moving slowly," Carlos complained. "There are people who can offer much cheaper prices, and I'm starting to think that we're out of our league."

"But you were the muthafucka that said you knew what you were doing, and it would be simple to get rid of the shit!" Roc yelled angrily.

People walking by looked at Roc as they passed by. "You better find a way to fix this shit, or else we're going to have all sorts of problems, and the drugs aren't going to be a part of it!"

"I'm working on it!" Carlos snapped. "Your ass better calm the fuck down before you end up having a stroke."

"That might be the solution to all of my problems. I'm on my way over there, and you better be ready to work off some of this stress," Roc demanded.

"I'm about to jump in the shower then. I'll have everything ready when you get here," Carlos assured him. "Tell me you love me."

"Fuck you!" Rock retorted, hanging up the phone.

He was too pissed at Carlos to say such a thing. If Carlos couldn't come up with a solution to their problem, he might have to do something desperate that he didn't even want to think about.

CJ and Precious were in an examining room, waiting for the doctor to come in to do an examination. Precious's morning sickness was getting worse, and she was having difficulty trying to hide it. Their prom and graduation went off without a hitch, and they both even got accepted into the colleges they had applied to. CJ suggested that they both select a school that was in St. Louis to make things simpler. He felt that just because Precious was pregnant, it didn't mean that they had to give up on their dreams. He had plans on eventually asking Precious to marry him by the time their child was five years old. He felt like they should be a legitimate family and didn't want his child to grow up without a father. Also, he wanted to do right by the both of them to make sure they lived a good life.

"I'm so nervous," Precious said, holding on tightly to CJ's hand.

"Everything is going to be okay," CJ assured her, kissing the back of her hand.

The door opened, and the doctor came inside. He had a pleasant smile on his face and noticed how nervous both Precious and CJ looked. This wasn't an unusual sight for him, because most new parents were always worried.

"How's it going?" Dr. Anderson asked pleasantly.

"I'm fine, Dr. Anderson," Precious replied. "This is my baby daddy, CJ. He's going to be coming to the appointments with me from now on."

"How are you, CJ?" Dr. Anderson asked.

"I'm okay… a little nervous but okay," CJ replied.

"I take it this is your first child as well," Dr. Anderson mentioned.

"Yes, sir," CJ replied. "This is the first one for the both of us, and we plan on having a few more."

Precious looked at him strangely.

"I don't know about all of that. We have to get through this first pregnancy before we start making plans for more kids," Precious added. "This morning sickness is no joke, and I figured it would be over by now."

"Some women experience morning sickness a lot longer than others. No pregnancy is the same, and it varies with each individual person," Dr. Anderson explained. "Today, we're going to do an NT scan to measure the baby's head and the thickness of the baby's neck."

"It's not going to hurt the baby is it?" CJ questioned.

"No, it's not going to hurt the fetus," Dr. Anderson assured him. "Have you been taking your prenatal vitamins, Precious?"

"Yes, I've been taking those horse pills," she replied, rolling her eyes up in her head. "I throw them back up, but I take them. I don't think this baby likes food."

"It will pass. I promise," Dr. Anderson assured her. "However, it is important that you stay hydrated, especially in all of this heat. If you can't keep food down, at least try to eat what's called a brat diet."

"What's that?" CJ asked curiously.

"It's called a brat diet because it consists of bananas, rice, apple sauce, and toast. Those are foods that people can sometimes stomach without them coming back up. The bananas are full of potassium, which is something that's good for both you and the baby."

"I like bananas," Precious mentioned. "And can I eat fried rice? Does that count?"

"You can eat fried rice, but it's high in sodium, and that's not good for you or the baby. Salt can lead to hypertension and other problems," Dr. Anderson explained. "White rice is the better option."

"Dang! I love me some chicken fried rice," Precious complained.

"You can eat it, but do it in moderation," Dr. Anderson replied, chuckling.

He continued to give her some more options while he washed his hands to prepare for the scan. He continued to ask Precious questions about her pregnancy and gave advice on things she should be doing to help make her pregnancy go smoothly. CJ was excited and taking in all of the information. After the exam, he and Precious took a few selfies to mark the occasion. They were keeping a visual diary in Precious's phone for the baby and planned on sharing it with their friends and family once they were ready to tell everyone. CJ took Precious to her favorite restaurant and got her some wings and fries. She probably was going to throw it all up, but that was neither here nor there. He wanted to make sure that she was getting enough to eat and that Precious was happy.

CJ dropped Precious off and was about to pull off when Trey came running out of the house, calling his name. He hadn't heard from Pooh in over a week, and they were supposed to be getting up on some lick that Pooh was working on. Trey knew that CJ didn't like Pooh and wanted nothing to do with him but thought maybe CJ might have seen him around the hood.

"Damn, nigga! I know you heard me calling your name," Trey said, panting. "Yo' ass been acting really funny lately. What? You don't fuck with your homie no more?"

"You know I've been working for my uncle and his partner, so don't even come to me like that," CJ replied defensively. "Plus, I told you I don't fuck with that nigga Pooh after he robbed me. I know you were the one who told him what I was doing, and I don't fuck around with snake ass niggas."

"So I'm a snake ass nigga now?"

"If the shoe fits, then wear it, nigga!" CJ snapped. "I was going to try to put you on once I got in the door good, but you fucked all of that up. I have to ride around with my uncle Usian now, and I don't have any freedom to do shit."

"Damn... that's fucked up," Trey replied, unphased. "I didn't tell Pooh exactly what you did for your uncle. I mentioned that you were being put on by Usian and soon would be able to hook us up."

"You know that nigga Pooh robs people, so I don't know why you would tell that nigga shit," CJ replied defensively. "I trusted you because you were my boy, and look at how you played me. Your sister is my gal, and how does it look when I have to tell her I don't fuck with you for real? You know she's going to side with me since she doesn't like Pooh's ass either."

"Y'all got my dude pegged all wrong. It was foul of him to rob you, but that's the way the game goes," Trey replied nonchalantly.

"Is that right? You should keep that same energy when you fully understand that I don't fuck with you," CJ replied.

He put his car in drive and pulled off. Usian had bought him a used Dodge Charger for graduation because he was proud of his accomplishment. Trey figured that CJ was out here eating good since he was riding around in a new car, and if he wasn't going to break bread with him, then maybe he and Pooh would have to hit CJ's ass up again but this time for all of his shit.

CHAPTER

Subira and Nika went to Meme's shop to see Usia. Zaida reached
out to Subira and confided in her about the financial situation
going on at their house. Zaida informed her that Jumba and Usia were up
to their eyeballs in debt and really needed the money that was promised to
them. Zaida even mentioned that Jumba said she would either have to start
paying rent or get her own place to live. Zaida has never lived alone, so
that was scary for her to hear. She pleaded with Subira to give them the
money, or else things were going to get worst. Subira told Zaida that she
would give Jumba and Usia the money only if Zaida agreed to move in
with her. She told Zaida that she was a vibrant, young woman that needed
to start living her best life. Zaida was in her mid-thirties and never dated,
but Subira wanted her sister to find a husband and enjoy the rest of her
years happy.

Subira and Nika walked into the shop and greeted everyone cheerfully.
The place was busy, and all of the braiders were with customers, doing
various styles of braids. Meme came over and greeted them with hugs.
Meme was always happy to see her sister and niece, and after what
happened at her party, she was eager to hear how things were going
between Nika and Usian. Nika pulled Meme away from Subira, and they
went into Meme's office. Subira scanned the braiding stations and noticed
one of the women had on a full hijab that covered her complete face. She
didn't have a client, and it appeared that she was reading a book. Subira
studied the head covering for a moment and realized it was Usia sitting

there, fully covered. She wondered if Jumba was making her wear it as a way of shaming her for what had happened, but either way, she was about to find out what was going on.

"I would like to speak to you for a moment," Subira said, closing the curtain behind her.

Usia turned to see Subira standing behind her and quickly turned back around. Subira was the last person she wanted to see or speak with right now because she knew how reactive her little sister could be. Subira already threatened to cut Jumba's hand off, so she might make good on the threat after all.

"We don't have anything to talk about," Usia replied softly. "You and your daughter have done plenty. I don't need any more problems in my household."

"Why are dressed like that?" Subira asked intently.

"Because I have been shamed by my husband," Usia replied defensively.

Subira walked over to her sister and grabbed at the bottom of Usia's hijab. She grabbed Subira's hand and tried to keep her from lifting it up, but she was too late. Subira yanked it up over Usia's face, and what she saw instantly brought tears to her eyes. Both of Usia's eyes were black and blue. There were bruises on her cheeks and forehead, and her lip was swollen and cut. Subira could tell that the marks were old and healing, but it still made her absolutely furious.

"I'm going to kill that fat muthafucka!" Subira declared through gritted teeth. "He did this to you, didn't he? How could he do this to your beautiful face?"

"It's… It's not what you think, Subira," Usia replied nervously. "I was attacked by some racist men who were trying to pull my hijab off of my head. I tried to fight them off, but there were too many of them."

"I don't believe you, Usia," Subira quickly replied. "Why are you defending that monster? I know that he puts his hands on you, Usia. This is not the first time he's done this to you!"

"You don't know what you're talking about, Subira," Usia protested. "Jumba loves me, and sometimes, I can do things that aren't aligned with what he wants."

"I don't care! That still doesn't give him the right to put his hands on you! I can't believe you're sitting up here, lying to me and defending that monster. It's obvious that he doesn't give a fuck about his family, because he was willing to sell his own flesh and blood out! Jumba only gives a fuck about himself and no one else!"

"That's not true, Subira. Jumba loves me and his family; I know it!"

Subira stared at her sister enraged because it hurt her heart to see Usia battered and bruised in such a matter. Tears ran down her cheeks, and Usia watched helplessly as she began to cry. She stood up and approached Subira, wiping her tears away. She hugged her sister tightly as they both wept in each other's arms.

"Jumba was so angry about what happened when we arrived home. He ranted and raved in the car the entire ride, and at one point, I thought we were going to get into a car accident. Zaida and the children were quiet, and I know it was scaring all of them. I tried to calm him down and change the subject, but it only upset him more," Usia explained. "As soon as we got into the house and up to our bedroom, he came after me so viciously. He punched me in my face, knocking me to the floor. He shouted obscenities and other malicious things at me while he continued to brutally punch me like I was nothing."

"I'm so sorry, Usia. I didn't expect this to happen," Subira apologized. "I would have done things differently if I'd known the coward was going to put his hands on you. The reason I came here today was to give you a check for the amount that was promised to Jumba. However, after seeing your face, I don't know if I want to give him anything."

"It really isn't all of his fault. Jumba has tried to provide the best life for us and our children. We've been taking care of Zaida since we came to the United States, and it has been a burden on us. We don't ask her for any money, and she gives us a few dollars to help out, but we do provide food and shelter for her."

"You won't have to worry about Zaida anymore, because she's moving out of your house. I asked her to move in with me since Nika will be living downstairs with her husband."

"I mean… she doesn't have to move out of our home, Subira. Jumba was frustrated that we weren't getting the money that was promised to us."

"It is time for Zaida to come out from under you and live the life Allah wants her to have. Zaida is still young and vibrate, and it is time for her to find a life of her own. You said it yourself that she's a bit of a burden on your family, so she's coming to live with me, and that's the end of it," Subira stated frankly.

Subira reached into her purse and pulled out an envelope. She handed it to Usia and then wrapped her arms around her sister's neck, hugging her tightly. She knew that she couldn't convince Usia to leave her husband, but she could love her sister from a distance and protect her by giving them the money.

"Take the check and give it to Jumba. I'm doing this more so for you, Usia, and the children. Fuck your husband and everything that he stands for," Subira uttered.

"Thank you," Usia whispered softly as tears ran down her face again. "But please don't be mad at Jumba. He's a man of principle and integrity—"

"Don't feed me that bullshit, Usia! He's a fucking pig that doesn't deserve to breathe! Any man that puts his hands on a defenseless woman and marks her face in such a manner is an animal! I hate him with all of my heart and soul, but he will have to face judgment when he dies, and I pray that Allah is not merciful! He deserves to die a thousand times and have his body desecrated by vultures and crows!"

"Please don't speak such ill intentions towards my husband!" Usia begged. "You don't understand, Usia, because Abdalla died early into your marriage. Do you think you would have lived such a free lifestyle if he were alive? I remember a time when you did as you were told and was just like me."

"I've never been a fool for Abdalla. I did what I was told and never talked back to him, but he did let me voice my opinion openly, and he did not beat me!" Subira said angrily. "How dare you try to compare your monster with my husband. They do share the same blood and were delivered by the same woman, but Jumba will *never* be half the man Abdalla was in life and in death!"

"I wasn't trying—"

"Yes you were, Usia," Subira said, cutting her off again. "Please take this check in good faith, and tell your good-for-nothing ass husband to stay the hell away from my family! The one fact that you may not know about my new son-in-law, he's a killer, and I won't hesitate to ask him to fuck Jumba up if he ever puts his hands on you again! You make sure you pass that on when you give his pathetic ass that check."

Subira kissed the top of her big sister's head and walked out of the Usia's station. She knew the check wasn't going to help change the situation between Usia and her husband. However, it would take some of the pressure off of their marriage. Jumba always hated that he lived in his big brother's shadow, but to have Subira be in control over all of her own affairs was the biggest slap in the face that Abdalla could have given him.

CHAPTER

Five

"Oh my God, Nika. You should have seen everyone's face when your mother stormed into the celebration and told them that you were now married to Usian," Meme said, laughing. "I thought Jumba was going to have a heart attack right there in the place. Baraka tried to act all big and bad, telling Subira that he didn't believe her. He told her that a marriage license needed to be produced, but when she pulled out that handkerchief, all of their mouths fell open."

"I wanted to be there to see it, but I needed to stay with Usian. Someone tried to kidnap him as he was leaving the lounge, and he got hurt in the process," Nika explained.

"He didn't get hurt badly, did he?"

"No," Nika replied, looking away. "He was sore from being grazed by a bullet in the shoulder, and his head was still hurting a bit by the time he arrived at the hotel. I wanted to go down there and beat the shit out of Roc. He's the only idiot that would try some stupid shit like that."

"Where would he get an idea like that from though?" Meme asked, sounding confused.

"I know... I know exactly where he got that stupid ass idea from," Nika fussed. "He got it from one of those dumb ass movies we used to watch all the time on Netflix. Roc was obsessed with watching all those hood movies with drug dealers, robbers, and killers. He used to crack me up, trying to imitate them with the way he dressed and acted. You should have seen his ass when we went out. He would have on all of these big ass chains and flashy jewelry. I believe his best friend sells drugs, and everyone assumes that Roc does as well."

"Now if that ain't some foolishness," Meme said, laughing. "Roc don't know shit about being in the streets. His ass grew up out in West county where the majority of their neighbors are doctors, lawyers, and business owners."

"We both know this, but I don't think the people hanging out in the lounges knew. People were treating him like he was a big deal when he took me to this lounge that Carlos frequented. I remember hearing two women talking about Roc being from Chicago, if I'm not mistaken. I started to correct them but decided against it. It was best to leave them in their ignorant bliss."

"I would have got their asses straight! I would have told them that 'this nigga here ain't from no Chicago,' and I would have given them a stank ass look, too!" Meme said boldly.

Nika looked at her aunt and laughed heartily. She loved having conversations with her crazy aunt. Meme was the only person who fully understood Nika, and Nika could go to her to talk about any and everything. Meme was more like a big sister than an aunt. "So let me ask you a question, Nika."

"Sure, what's up?"

"How has the sex been between you and your husband? I know he tore that little puss up when he first popped your cherry!" Meme teased, laughing.

"Oh my God, Meme!" Nika shouted, giggling. "You're wrong for that! You know it hurts like a son of a gun! I tried to be a big girl about the situation, and Usian was being as gentle as possible."

"Give me details, hunty! I want to know all the bloody details, and don't skip a beat," Meme declared. "You know I have to know all of the tea so that I can go back and tell yo' mama."

"You be telling my mama what we talk about?" Nika asked, looking mortified.

"I don't tell her verbatim, but we do have conversations surrounding issues pertaining to you," Meme explained. "However, I don't tell her the juicy stuff. I keep all of those details to myself. I didn't tell her that Usian was sucking on you, and I knew about that for a while."

Nika let out a sigh of relief. The mere thought of Meme telling her mother some of the stuff she'd discussed with Meme had her more embarrassed than when Subira found out that she had been sneaking downstairs to lay with Usian. She trusted her auntie with all of her secrets and knew better than to think that Meme would tell Subira everything. "So come with it, suga, and tell me all of the good stuff before your mama comes into the office and interrupts us. I know your ass ain't going to want to talk when she appears, so stop stalling and spill the beans!"

Nika was happy to oblige her aunt and went into detail about the entire evening. She told her about the chastity belt that Subira made her put on and how Usian seemed to be excited about it. She explained how she'd given her first blow job to Usian and how Kimmie taught her how to do it using popsicles and porno movies. Meme cracked jokes and teased Nika about the things she was saying, and both women laughed hysterically. However, Nika got serious when she expressed her lack of experience with sex. She wasn't sure if Usian was satisfied with her performance at all. There was nothing for her to gauge her performance, and this made her a bit subconscious when it came to making love to her husband.

"Nika, I'm sure Usian is enjoying your virginal grip. You have every right to feel self-conscious about your performance because you don't have any experience and Usian has plenty, but that shit doesn't matter to a man who loves you. Usian will teach you how to satisfy him without you even realizing that it's being done."

"Are you talking about when he asked me to loosen my grip when I'm jacking him off?" Nika asked shyly. "He told me I had a Kungfu grip and that I needed to choke the chicken, not strangle it."

Meme fell out, laughing at her niece. She dropped her head on her desk as she laughed hysterically. Nika didn't find it funny at first, but the way her auntie was laughing, she ended up laughing herself. "Stop laughing at me, Auntie!" Nika insisted, laughing. "You know I'm used to gripping these bald-headed ass women's edges that are barely there, so my grasp is a bit strong."

"Nika, yo' ass is crazy!" Meme declared. "How can you even compare the two? Ha… ha… ha… ha… ha… ha…"

"See, Auntie, that's why I'm done talking to you," Nika said, taking her phone out of her pocket.

—It was vibrating against her leg, and she wanted to see who was calling. "This is my husband!" she said excitedly. "Excuse me for a second."

Nika got up and stepped out of the office. Subira was on her way to get Nika and stepped inside of Meme's office when she saw Nika headed in the other direction. She was all bubbly and giggly, so Subira knew that Usian was the one on the phone. She loved how he made her daughter happy, and she prayed that things continued on a positive path.

"Hey, sissy! How's it going?" Meme asked, smiling brightly.

"I don't know," Subira replied wearily. "Did you see what that bastard did to our sister's face?"

Meme looked at Subira suspiciously.

"I knew her ass was lying," Meme uttered, sounding frustrated. "She told me that a group of men attacked her because she had on a hijab."

"She tried that shit with me, but I knew her ass was lying," Subira replied irritably. "Because if some shit like that happened in real life, Jumba would have been the first person on national television, trying to campaign for some sympathy. You know his greedy ass is shameless when it comes to money."

"Ohhhh... you're mad mad," Meme replied, getting hype. "We should go whoop his fat ass!"

"I agree, Meme, but it's not our fight," Subira replied solemnly. "You know, in our religion, we are viewed as property to our husbands to do whatever they see fit. I've always been outspoken, and that's why my husband desired me so much. My Nika has both her father and my spirit inside of her, and Usian understands that Nika is not going to be controlled. She agreed to be submissive to him, but she will not be a fool nor a slave for him."

"That's good to hear. I'm glad that Nika let Usian know upfront where she's coming from. Nika had an advantage that neither one of us had. Our husbands were selected for us, but I'm glad that Hanif was selected for me. Usian reminds me of him a little. They both know how to handle the crazy Okonjo women," Meme said, laughing.

Nika came back into the office while her mother and aunt were laughing. She wondered if the joke was at her expense, so she had a blank expression on her face. Meme had been cracking jokes and mocking her the entire time they were conversing. Nika also knew that Meme couldn't hold water when it came to Subira, so she wondered what piece of her business Meme had told Subira now.

"What are y'all laughing at?" Nika asked defensively.

Both women looked at Nika strangely and continued laughing. "I know y'all in here talking and laughing at me. What did you tell Mama, Meme?"

"Girl... ain't nobody stuttin' yo' ass," Meme replied, chuckling. "There are other things for me and my sister to talk about besides you. However, if you want to go there... Subira, your daughter has a Kungfu grip!"

Nika's eyes grew wide while Meme laughed uncontrollably. The embarrassment on Nika's face made Subira start laughing, and eventually, Nika joined in. They continued to laugh as they talked about being married. Meme and Subira even shared their stories about their first time being with their husbands, and Nika took all of it in. She no longer felt so self-conscious about her sex game with Usian, but there would still be some insecurity present until she fully learned how to satisfy her husband without his assistance. Nika was overjoyed with the amount of sex they were having because even though she wasn't sure of herself, it still felt wonderful when they did it.

CHAPTER

*N*ika was home, cooking dinner for Usian, while he was out helping her mother. He had left with Subira to go help move Zaida's stuff to their house. Subira had explained to Nika that Jumba had beaten up Usia and talked about the so-called burden that Zaida had become. Nika was upset that Jumba had done such a thing and offered to go over there with her mother to jump on her uncle. Usian wasn't too happy to hear about what had happened either when it was explained to him and stated that he would kill Jumba if he'd ever laid hands on Nika or Subira.

Nika decided to straighten up around the house while her dinner continued to cook. She had made some baked whiting fillets with twice baked potatoes, broccoli, and garlic bread. She wanted to show off her cooking skills since Subira was always the one sending him food. She swept and mopped the floor in the kitchen and cleaned the bathroom, which was a battle within itself. Living with two men was going to be a challenge because them remembering to lower the toilet seat had become a fight that she was continuously losing. The addition of bleach tablets in the toilet helped sanitize it to her liking, but the piss stains on the rim and in front of the toilet were two things that she only wished would go away on their own.

Nika was on her way to the living room when she walked past CJ's room and noticed the door was open. She peeked inside, noticing a bunch of dishes randomly all over the place and decided to go get them so that they could be washed and put away in their proper places. Nika instantly started kicking clothes over to one side of the room. She picked up stray bowls, plates, cups, and silverware off his chest, nightstand, and floor, which was totally disgusting. She noticed there were a lot more to get on the other side of the room, and this drove her crazy! Nika went over to his desk and grabbed a tall stack of dishes off of it. She noticed a piece of paper with the SSM insignia on it. Her brow furrowed as she thumbed through and read the information on the sheet. Precious's name was all over the paperwork, and it stated that she was ten weeks pregnant. Nika was in shock from what she'd read and didn't hear CJ coming into the house. She jumped when she looked up and saw him in the doorway. A glass that she was holding slipped out of her hand and fell to the floor. It shattered into several pieces all over the place, causing Nika to panic.

"Shit!" Nika called out. "How the hell did that happen?"

"Are you alright?" CJ asked, rushing over to her. "Watch your step when you move out of the way."

He went over to the spot where she'd dropped the glass and started picking up the pieces. "I'm sorry if I scared you, Nika. I learned at an early age not to make too much noise when I move around the house. My mama used to cuss us out if we made too much noise, walking through her house."

"I think it's a black thing because my mama used to tell me not to walk so hard on the floor. We used to have this old lady that lived down here, and she would tell my mama that it sounds like I was coming through the floor when I walked," Nika recalled, laughing.

"I got knocked upside my head one time for waking my little brother up when he was a baby," CJ mentioned. "She used to knock the hell out of us on GP it felt like sometimes."

CJ got quiet for a moment while he picked up the last of the bigger pieces. "I miss that—her cursing me out."

"Usian told me some stories about your mother, and it sounds like she was off the chain," Nika said, walking past CJ. "Let me go put these dishes in the sink and grab a broom."

Nika quickly went into the kitchen and set the dishes down in the sink. Her thoughts were running rapidly because she didn't know what to say to CJ. A part of her wanted to ask him if Precious was in fact pregnant. The paper said it clearly, but maybe they were planning to get an abortion or something. They both got into two good schools, and they both were talking like nothing was going to keep them from going to school. Nika grabbed the broom and dustpan out the broom closet and headed back to CJ's room. She stopped at the door and took a few deep breaths before she entered back into the room. Nika didn't want to seem nervous or anxious around CJ; more importantly, she was nervous and anxious about mentioning this to Usian because she wasn't sure how he would respond to the news.

"Nika, did you happen to read these papers on my desk?" CJ asked nonchalantly.

"What papers?" Nika replied, trying to play it off. "There's so much junk on your desk, and those dishes were taking up all kinds of space."

Nika started to sweep up the remaining shards of glass in hopes that CJ would drop the subject.

"Nika, I know you read the paper because you're acting strange as hell," CJ said, plopping down on his bed. "Please don't tell Usian. I want to be the one to tell him man to man."

"That's fine by me," Nika quickly replied. "I'm scared for your ass truthfully though."

She looked at CJ and chuckled a bit. "You know that nigga is bipolar, and I don't want him getting mad at me for knowing before him."

"Do you think he's going to be mad?" CJ asked sincerely. "I mean, I've graduated out of high school, and both me and Precious are going to college. I'm trying to save up enough money for us to move into our own apartment because I know we can't stay here since the two of you are married, and Precious's mama is going to put her out as soon as she starts showing."

"When do you plan on telling him, CJ? It's not good for me to keep secrets from Usian. He's my husband now, and it's my duty to be open and honest with him. I can't be keeping secrets from mister."

"I understand what you're saying, but I really need for you to not say anything, Nika," CJ pleaded.

He thought for a second while Nika stared at him uncomfortably. "How about I tell him sometime next week?" CJ offered. "I just need to make sure some things are squared away before I tell him."

"I don't know, CJ," Nika replied wearily. "A good marriage is built on trust, and I don't want my marriage to start off on a bad note."

"I will take full responsibility. I promise you," CJ assured her with pleading hands. "Give me another week, and I promise I will tell Usian that Precious is pregnant."

Nika stood silent for a few more seconds before she responded. She knew the right thing to do was to tell Usian about the pregnancy, but her heart was telling her to grant CJ his wish, even though it may cause problems between her and Usian.

"Okay, fine, CJ. I'm not going to say anything to Usian about Precious being pregnant, but you better tell him next week, or else I'm going to spill all of your business," Nika informed him.

CJ looked at her excitedly and jumped up off the bed. He grabbed Nika and hugged her tightly while continuously thanking her. Whether she knew it or not, she had put to bed a lot of anxiety that CJ was just feeling. He had a feeling that Nika could be persuaded to go his way, but she could be a wild card at times. CJ let Nika go, and she walked out of the room to go check on her food. CJ decided to go into the kitchen and clean all of his dirty dishes while he and Nika talked about life.

It was a little after eleven o'clock when Usian came home. He had gone to run an errand with Whisper after dropping off Zaida's stuff at the house. They had gotten a lead on the car that the two men were in that tried to kidnap him. Usian refused to let the situation drop because he wanted to know if Roc was behind it. He had heard Subira and Zaida talking about what happened in Usia's house when they arrived home from the celebration.

Subira had mentioned that her big sister's face looked like she had been beaten badly, and Usian didn't agree with that. The worse thing a man could do was beat on a defenseless woman. He offered to go lay hands on Jumba after he put the last box in the back of his pickup truck. However, Subira told Usian that it wasn't necessary, because it would be a waste of time. She knew Usia would never forgive her, and Jumba would find another way to punisher her for it.

The cycle of abuse was sometimes more mental than people realized. It was easy to say that a person could break away from someone, but when you genuinely loved and cared about someone, you couldn't easily escape the things that bound you together. Usia grew up in a religion where her husband's word was the law of the land, and it was customary for her to obey his commands. Usian vowed to himself that he wouldn't be that type of husband to Nika. Besides, she wouldn't let him get it off anyway.

Usian walked into the house and went straight back to the kitchen. Nika had texted him earlier to say that his dinner was wrapped up and on the stove in case she was upstairs when he arrived home. She was spending time with her mother and aunt, helping Zaida get settled into her new home. Subira and Nika went out and bought new furniture, curtains, and artwork for the walls. They wanted Zaida to feel like she was coming to her own room instead of moving into Nika's.

Usian stood at the kitchen sink, washing his hands. He thought about the young dude that he'd smacked around, trying to get information from him. Usian was surprised that the big-mouthed dude didn't have too much to say, considering his ass always seemed to know everything that was going on in the streets. Maybe dude was more afraid of the person in question, or he simply didn't know anything.

Usian shut off the water and grabbed a paper towel off the wall. He wiped his hands as he walked over to the stove and grabbed his food. He took the foil off the top of it and put it in the microwave right above him. He pressed a number and walked back over to the sink to grab a fork to eat with. He hoped that Nika remembered to put some sodas in the refrigerator because he could sure go for an ice cold Vess pineapple right about now with this delicious smelling meal heating up. The one thing he asked Nika to always do was to keep his three favorite drinks cold in the refrigerator. That was bottled water, some type of soda, and beer. That was an easy request that Nika has managed to get praised for. She learned his likes and dislikes easily and shopped in bulk at the grocery store. Usian liked her style and loved going shopping with Nika. It was a way for them to spend time together, and he could see how much money his wife was spending every time she swiped her card.

Usian opened the fridge and smiled when he saw the sleeves of sodas sitting on the shelf. There were three flavors to choose from, and that made Usian very happy. He grabbed a pineapple soda out of the box and closed the door behind him. His phone dinged, alerting him that he had a text message, so he pulled it out of his pocket. He looked down at the screen and rolled his eyes at the message. He swiped the screen and deleted it because he didn't want any shit from his wife. He had made it perfectly clear to Jessica that he didn't want her at all, in any type of way. He thought it was considerate of him to tell her face to face that he was married to Nika now, but it seemed like that fueled her even more. Usian didn't put his hands on women, but he might have to pay Ew Baby a few dollars to beat Jessica's ass.

Usain took his food out of the microwave and brought it over to the table. He sat down to enjoy this nice meal that his wife made for him before going to take a shower and getting in bed to make love to her. He loved being able to slow grind in her soft, tight, wet folds. That was the one place that felt like heaven to him, and it was the only place that he wanted to be. Marrying Nika was the best decision that he'd ever made, and it was a choice that he'd make time and time again. He dug his fork into his vegetables when Nika walked into the kitchen. She was wearing one of his wife beaters and looked sexy as hell to Usian.

"Damn, baby, you trying to poke a nigga's eye out with them big, hard ass nipples?" Usian teased when Nika bent over to plant a kiss on his forehead. "I should put that muthafucka in my mouth."

"You so silly," Nika replied, pushing his head. "Eat your dinner, and we'll get to that in a minute. It's after eleven o'clock, and you were supposed be here hours ago."

"I know, baby, but it took us a little longer than we expected," Usian explained. "I have a hard time believing niggas when they tell me shit, so I might keep hitting they ass until he tells me something."

"Is that why your knuckles are swollen and scrapped up?" Nika asked, walking over to the refrigerator. "Why didn't you wear gloves or something? You're not going to rub those rough ass joints against my soft, smooth skin. It'll look like I have bike paths etched out on my ass like I got a map tattooed on me or something."

Usian stopped eating and almost choked from the way Nika responded to him. He laughed as she walked over to him and placed an ice pack on the back of his right hand. She stocked up on those as well because Usian had come in the house a bunch of late nights with bruised and swollen knuckles. She stocked up on Ace bandages as well since this appeared to be a pattern. Nika didn't ask any questions and only did her wifely duties, but Usian would always confide in his wife, and she allowed herself to be his refuge.

However, she only wished that Usian trusted her enough to be honest and truthful about Jessica. Nika knew that Jessica had been trying to get in contact with him because she had seen old text messages from her when they first got married. Nika thought they were going to stop when Usian told her that he was married, but it has seemed to have gotten worse. Jessica even tried to say that she was pregnant, but there was no way that Usian could be the father since he's stopped fucking her a long time ago. She didn't want to be a jealous wife, but sometimes, you could only take so much. Nika wasn't exactly a pushover, and if she needed to step in and say something to Jessica, she'd check her thoroughly like a federal government checklist at the Mexican border.

CHAPTER

Tap... tap... tap... tap...

Usian lifted his head off the pillow and looked around the room. He laid back down and nestled his body against Nika's to go back to sleep. He thought maybe the birds were outside, trying to fix their nest. *Tap... tap... tap... tap...*

"What the hell is that?" Nika moaned, readjusting herself on the pillow. "If it's those birds out there, tripping, you're going to have to remove that nest in the morning."

"I don't know if that's the birds," Usian replied. "It sounds like someone tapping on the window with something."

Boom... boom... boom... boom... Usian sat straight up and wiped his eyes. Now, that sounded like someone beating on the front door, and he couldn't understand why. He looked over at the clock, and it was after three o'clock in the morning. He knew it wasn't CJ, because he would have called his phone if he didn't have his key.

"Who the fuck is that beating on the door like they crazy?" Nika asked, lifting up.

"I don't know, but I'm about to find out," Usian said, grabbing his shorts off the floor.

"I'm about to come see too!" Nika said, reaching over to grab her tank top.

"You keep your ass right here in the bed," Usian ordered. "I'll go see who it is."

Usian grabbed his gun off the nightstand and headed toward the door. He doubled back to put on his slides then proceeded to go to the front of the house. When he approached the door, whoever was knocking began to beat on the door again. Usian unlocked the deadbolt and handle then swung the door open. He had a mean grimace on his face and was pissed off when he saw Jessica's ass standing in front of him.

"Why the fuck is you beating on my door like you're crazy or something at three o'clock in the morning?" Usian said angrily.

"Because you didn't come to the window when I was tapping on it," Jessica replied, giggling. "I was hoping that we could have a little fun like old times. I know that you're married now, but she can get in on it too. I remember how much you used to like to have threesomes with me and my friends."

"Look, Jessica, I don't know what type of shit you're on, but you better get the fuck away from my door with that bullshit!" Usian demanded. "I told your ass several times that I wasn't fucking with you anymore. I don't know what part of that you can't understand!"

"But I love you, Usian! You can't just throw me away because suddenly you're all in love with the bitch from upstairs! I loved you first, and she's going to have to accept the fact that I'm a part of your life! We can share that big dick… You know how to satisfy two women at the same damn time!"

Jessica grabbed at the screen door, but it was still locked. She looked up at Usian with her brow furrowed while he scowled at her. She couldn't understand why Usian was acting this way with her. In Jessica's eyes, Usian knew that she loved him, and how could he go off and marry someone else, knowing that she cared so deeply for him? "Open the fucking door, Usian, and stop being so difficult!" Jessica demanded. "You're acting like a bitch ass nigga!"

"Go the fuck home, Jessica!" Usian ordered. "You're drunk and making a fool out of yourself."

"No I'm not!" Jessica shouted angrily. "Now open this fucking door!"

Nika could hear everything that was going on in the front of the house, and it was pissing her off. She had noticed several text messages on Usian's phone from Jessica a few days ago, and she even saw a few missed calls on his call log. She didn't want to be one of those wives that didn't trust her husband, but Nika was still rather insecure when it came to Usian. He assured her that she was the only woman he had eyes for and that he'd never cheat on her. However, the way women swooned over him when they went to the lounge made Nika feel some type of way. She never used to notice it since they never went to the Gateway together, but now that they were married, it seemed like all the women were coming out of the woodworks at him.

Nika got up out of the bed and put her tank top on. She grabbed a pair of shorts that she wore around the house and put on a pair of tennis shoes. She laced them up tightly with the intent to put in some work. Nika refused to be disrespected, especially at her own home.

"Usiannnnn… why are you doing me like this?" Jessica cried out. "I love you… and… and… you know this, so why are you treating me like shit? I'm surrendering myself to you wholeheartedly! I worship the ground that you walk on, and I will be your personal love slave. Your wife doesn't have to know about it!"

"Bitch… you've gone too far now!" Nika said, pushing Usian out of the way. "Get the fuck away from our door, or else I'm going to come out there and beat the fuck out of you!"

"Nika, I got this," Usian said, grabbing her arm.

"Apparently, you ain't got shit if this bitch is still standing at our door, crying and making a fool out of herself," Nika replied angrily. "It's three o'clock in the morning, and this disrespectful bitch is going to wake up the entire house! I don't need my mama coming downstairs and questioning me about an irrelevant ass bitch!"

"Who are you calling irrelevant?" Jessica shot back. "Bitch, you're the one who's irrelevant! Usian is only doing this because he's mad at me! I should have been honest with you about Jabari from the beginning. I was wrong for trying to get back at him with you, but I love you, Usian… I don't love Jabari!"

"Bitch, I ain't never loved you, nor have I ever expressed to you that I do," Usian insisted. "We had a fuck thing going on, and I ain't going to lie, I enjoyed your sex, but that's all that it was between us."

"You're lying! That's not true, Usian! You know that you love me!" Jessica shouted, outraged.

"Get the fuck away from our door, hoe! My husband no longer wants to deal with you, and I'm about five seconds away from beating your ass!" Nika said, moving toward the door.

"Bitch, fuck you! Why don't you step out that door so I can beat your ass!" Jessica yelled. "You ain't shit special, and I'm going to get my man back!"

Nika tried to push past Usian again, but he grabbed her and wouldn't let her get to the screen door. He didn't want his wife out there fighting a woman who wasn't relevant, and besides, he didn't know if Nika knew how to handle herself. Jessica was a street chick that had been in plenty of fights. She might beat the shit out of Nika, and that wouldn't sit right with him.

"Let me go, Usian!" Nika yelled. "I'm going to beat this bitch's ass!"

"Let that hoe go." Jessica laughed. "I got something for this bitch!"

Nika snatched away from Usian and unlocked the screen door. She wasn't afraid, because her mother taught her how to defend herself. She took martial arts classes from the time she was five years old and was a black belt by the time she was ten years old.

"Yeah! Come on outside so I can show you something, bitch!" Jessica threatened.

She stepped back, throwing her purse down on the porch. She started taking off her earrings and other jewelry, throwing it down as well. She was stumbling a little, and Nika picked up on it as she came out of the door. This wasn't going to be a long fight, because Nika felt that Jessica was at a disadvantage.

"Come on and let's do this!" Jessica yelled, running toward Nika.

Nika planted her feet and swung her arm, hitting Jessica square in the bridge of her nose when she got close to Nika. Jessica stumbled backward and stopped, putting her hand up to her nose. She pulled it down, and there wasn't any blood present, but it stung really badly. This infuriated Jessica even more, so she rushed Nika again. Usian stepped out on the porch and stood close to where Nika was standing. Jessica ran up on Nika again, swinging her arms wildly, and Nika looked over at Usian like she couldn't believe it. When Jessica got close enough to Nika, she stuck her foot out and tripped Jessica, making her fall forward on the porch.

Nika was aware that Jessica was intoxicated, so she didn't want to take advantage of the situation. She walked over and grabbed Jessica by the hair and dragged her across the porch toward the steps. She pulled her down each one of them and made sure that Jessica felt all the discomfort that the steps offered. Jessica was kicking and screaming while Nika continued to drag her down the walkway toward the gate.

"Let this be a lesson to you, dumb bitch, not to come around here anymore," Nika said through gritted teeth.

She opened the gate then grabbed two handfuls of Jessica's hair and swung her onto the sidewalk. Next, Nika walked out onto the sidewalk and stood over Jessica. She wanted to let her know that she wouldn't be so nice next time.

"I spared you this time, hoe!" Nika said, hitting Jessica in the face. "The next time you show up at my house uninvited—no matter what the time is—I'm going to dog walk your ass to the point where someone will have to pry your ass up off the ground in order for you to leave. Do I make myself clear?" Nika grabbed and pulled at her hair for emphasis. "Do you hear me!" Nika shouted.

She hit Jessica in the face a few more times, and Jessica yelled out in agreement. Usian chuckled as he picked up Jessica's shit and walked down the path to go get his wife. His dick was harder than Superman's elbow from watching Nika get down on Jessica. He was so used to hearing Nika go off on people that he assumed she really wasn't a fighter. However, after seeing his wife in action, he would never underestimate her again.

"Come on, baby," Usian said, grabbing Nika's arm. "I think you got your point across."

"I think so too," Nika agreed.

"I didn't know you were so aggressive, and I must admit it turned me on," Usian said, collecting her in his arms.

"I can tell," Nika replied, giggling. "My best friend is sticking me in the leg."

"C'mon," Usian said, leading Nika toward the house.

Jessica was lying on the ground, crying hysterically as she watched Usian and Nika walk into their house. She was embarrassed and felt defeated by what had happened. She couldn't understand why Usian chose Nika over her, but she refused to accept it. There was no way that Usian would get rid of her this easily, and she would catch Nika one day to get revenge for her actions.

Usian and Nika walked into their bedroom and instantly attacked each other. Usian passionately kissed his wife while gripping two handfuls of her butt. Nika had her hands down in Usian's shorts, trying to free him. She had so much aggression built up inside of her that she needed to release. Usian kissed down her neck and sucked on it like a vampire before pushing her down on the bed.

"Take all of that shit off," Usian ordered. "I want to see you completely naked."

Nika did exactly what he asked and stripped all her clothes off her body. Usian did the same thing and watched his wife lustfully until every stitch of clothing was off her body. He leaned down, kissing her on the lips as she reciprocated with the same intensity. Usian kissed down her neck to her shoulder then latched on to one of her nipples. He sucked it relentlessly, causing Nika to arch her back. He moved over to the other one while rubbing his fingers against her sweet spot. Nika moaned uncontrollably as her husband played with her body. He knew exactly what to do to get her so wet, and Nika loved every minute of it. Usian pulled away and stared into Nika's eyes. He could tell she was worked up and horny just the way he liked it, and the tongue lashing he was about to give her was definitely going to have her screaming.

Usian kissed down Nika's stomach and made his way to her money spot. He licked up the crease of her folds before latching on to her clit. He sucked and beat his tongue against it, making Nika squirm in an attempt to get away. He grabbed both of her wrists and pinned them to the bed. He flickered his tongue against her bud before latching back on to it. He sucked hard, periodically dipping his tongue inside of her walls, and this drove Nika crazy.

"Fuck me, please!" she begged. "I want you inside of me!"

Usian ignored her cries and continued to feast on her goodness. Since they'd been married, Nika preferred to be fucked and doing all of the sucking. She felt empowered when she had all of the control, and she liked having her pussy pounded out by her husband several times a day. Usian ignored her cries and brought her to climax, causing Nika's entire body to shake. He lifted up and kissed her mouth passionately while Nika licked all of her essence off his lips. She reached down, grabbing his stiff erection, and rubbed the head at the crease of opening. She guided it inside of her and pushed down so that she could take as much of him as she could.

"You're greedy and impatient, baby. I was going to give it all to you," Usian said, chuckling.

"I knoooowwww..." Nika moaned, enjoying the feeling of his dick inside of her.

Usian continued to stroke her slow and steady as Nika marveled at the feeling. He was filling her insides with all of him, and she could never get enough. He quickened his pace and took her bottom lip into his mouth. He sucked on it hungrily as the feeling began to overwhelm him. He sped up his pace and dug deeper inside of her womb. Nika didn't object to it and wrapped her arms around his neck. Usian continued to pound her insides, and Nika called out in ecstasy.

Her pussy was getting wetter and wetter, and this was driving Usian crazy. He slid out of her and went back down in between her legs, eating her pussy hungrily. He licked, sucked, and fingered her goodness while Nika moaned and humped his face. He flipped Nika over on her stomach and pulled her up on her knees. He stood up off the bed and made her feet hang over the sides. Usian rubbed his stiffness against her wet folds then plunged his hard dick inside of wetness. He held his head back because her pussy gripped it like a glove. There was no way he could ever imagine being without this feeling for the rest of his life.

Usian grabbed Nika's hip with one hand and pushed deep inside of her, readjusting his grip on her hips. He pushed inside of her a few times before unleashing the fury within. He pounded her insides, causing Nika to cry out in pleasurable pain. They had never done this position before, but Nika found herself liking it. Usian continued to assault her insides, and Nika moaned in enjoyment.

"Whose pussy is this?" Usian growled in her ear.

"Ah shit, bae!" Nika screamed. "It's your pussy!"

"Make me know it!" Usian ordered. "Fuck me back, Nika."

She wasn't sure what he was asking, but she was determined to do it. She pushed back, meeting his strokes, and after a few times, he stopped and let her control their pace. Nika was slamming her ass back against him, and Usian was enjoying every minute of it.

"I'm about to cum," Nika uttered.

"Give it to me then," Usian replied, reaching down playing with her clit.

They continued to hump like two wild dogs until Nika screamed out in satisfaction. Her body went limp, and she collapsed on the bed, but Usian went down with her, making sure that he didn't come out. He still had to get his money and knew what to do to get it. He continued to long stroke his wife and picked up the pace because he felt himself about to nut.

"Give it all to me," Nika begged. "I want all your babies."

"As you wish," Usian whispered in her ear. "Ahhhh... man, damn!"

Usian released himself deep inside of Nika. She opened her legs wider and pushed back against him, making sure she received every drop that he had to offer. Usian kissed her shoulders softly before pulling out, then they cuddled up and then drifted off back to sleep.

ONE WEEK LATER...

Usian and Nika had date night after a long week of working. The Jessica incident was followed up with a lot of threatening phone calls and text messages to Usian's phone. He had blocked every number that she had called and messaged from, but it seemed like she wasn't running out of numbers. Jessica was pissed off at the aftereffects of Nika's punches the next morning when she looked in the mirror at her face. Also, she had several scrapes on her legs, arms, and back from Nika dragging her from the porch to the sidewalk. Jessica's entire body was sore, and she swore on her grandmother's life that she would get Nika back for the assault.

Usian was standing behind Nika while she unlocked the screen door. He stood really close to her, pressing himself against the crease of her butt. He planted small kisses on her neck, making Nika smile. His hands wandered her body, sliding all around her curves, and eventually, they landed on her breast. He cupped them and pinched her nipples through the fabric of her shirt and the lace of her bra.

Nika couldn't concentrate and kept attempting to put the key in the lock, but whenever she tried, Usian would hit one of her spots that caused her to lean back against him and moan uncontrollably. She pushed her butt out, grinding it into his semi-erect manhood. Usian moaned softly into her ear before turning her head to the side with his hand and kissed her. They tongued each other down nastily in the doorway while they continued to freak all over one another. If Nika didn't have on a long skirt that reached her feet, they would probably be in the doorway, fucking.

Nika turned around to face her husband with a lustful look in her eyes. She unfastened the button on his chinos and proceeded to stick her hand down in his pants. She gripped the girth of his rod and moved her hand vigorously up and down while sucking on his bottom lip. Cars were driving down the street, but neither one of them seemed to mind. Usian put both of his hands on Nika's face and pressed his lips firmly against hers. He breathed heavily into her mouth because her magical hand was working wonders. He wasn't ready to cum just yet, but if they kept up this pace they were going, he was going to explode all over her hand in a matter of minutes.

"You need to turn around and open the door, now!" Usian insisted. "I don't want to cum all over your hand and waste my load."

"I can get you back hard if that's what you're worried about," Nika teased. "I seem to have a certain effect over you."

"You're lucky that you have on that long ass disciple skirt because if you wore one of those little bitty ones, you would be bent over with this stiff one all up in them guts," Usian teased.

He kissed her cheek and squeezed her tightly. Nika stuck her key into the lock and opened the door. Usian pinched her butt, causing Nika to jump forward. She hurried into the house, and Usian was on her heels. He shut and locked the door behind him while Nika waited anxiously. He approached her slowly, and Nika was smitten by her husband. He stopped in front of her, spinning her around so that her back was against his chest. He pulled her skirt down with one good tug and made sure that her panties were with it. He bent her over the couch while his fingers rubbed against her folds. He slid them deep inside of her, and Nika shook as she let out a throaty moan. Usian's fingers went in and out of her rapidly, and she pumped them back. "Ohhh... baby, you're so wet," Usian uttered.

"Mmmm... hmmm..." Nika replied.

She started throwing it back even harder on his hand when she saw CJ's door come open. The light shown into the hallway, and a figure's shadow appeared on the wall. Nika stiffened her body and stood up straight. It caused Usian's fingers to come out of her wetness, pissing him off. His brow furrowed, and he looked up at her disapprovingly because he didn't tell her to move.

"What the fuck are you doing?" Usian asked hostilely.

Subira came out of the room, and a panicked look appeared on Nika's face.

"Mama! What are you doing down here?" Nika asked, pulling her skirt up in a hurry.

Subira turned around and squinted, trying to see where the voice was coming from.

"Nika, where are you?" Subira replied. "I can't see you."

Nika pushed past Usian, walking into the hallway where her mother stood. "There you are! What are you doing in the dark?"

"We just walked through the door," Nika explained, looking back Usian.

She fixed her disheveled clothing, wiping the sweat from her brow. Usian walked up to Nika and stood close behind her. His dick was still semi-erect as he pressed it against her butt. Nika quipped and took a step forward while Subira stared at them strangely.

"Mama, why are you down here?" Nika asked again.

"I asked her to come down here," CJ replied, stepping out of his room. "Precious isn't feeling well, and I didn't know what to do."

"That's no reason to go upstairs and disturb Ms. Subira," Usian replied, sounding annoyed.

Subira lifted an eyebrow at him. "I mean Mama. You know I have to get used to calling you that."

"I know," Subira replied, chuckling. "I'm messing with you."

Zaida came out of the room and stopped in the doorway.

"She needs to go to the hospital," Zaida announced in a serious tone. "She may be having a miscarriage, and that's why she's spotting."

"Oh my God!" CJ cried. "Can you take us, Nika?"

"Wait a minute!" Usian called out. "Who's having a miscarriage?"

"Precious," Subira replied. "You didn't know that she's pregnant? According to she and CJ, she's twelve weeks pregnant."

"I can explain!" CJ said nervously.

"You can explain!" Usian repeated. "Don't you think you should have done that shit sooner?"

CJ could tell that Usian was pissed off. He was supposed to tell him last week, but with the promise of possibly getting an apartment next week, he figured he could hold out on telling Usian. "And why are you asking Nika to take you to the hospital? You can take her by yourself."

"I'm too scared for us to go by ourselves," CJ replied.

"I'll go with you," Nika agreed. "Tell Precious to put her shoes on and let's go."

Usian was beyond pissed off because he knew something wasn't being said.

"Nika, did you know that Precious was pregnant?" Usian asked, looking at her accusingly.

Nika didn't answer at first, giving Usian the answer to his question. She had been acting weird this past week whenever Usian asked her any question about CJ or Precious. As a matter of fact, Nika would get defensive when she answered him, and that seemed strange. He knew that there was something she wasn't telling him, but he thought it had something to do with Precious stealing money from CJ. "You not answering is telling me everything I need to know. Why didn't you tell me that the girl was pregnant?"

"I made her promise not to tell you, Usian," CJ interjected. "I was supposed to tell you last week, but I had gotten a lead on this apartment I'm trying to rent. I wanted to be able to tell you that we were moving when I told you about the baby."

"For the record, I been told him to tell you," Precious said, walking out of the room. "Your nephew is petrified of you and finds it difficult to talk to you about anything."

"That's ridiculous! CJ, you know you can talk to me about whatever," Usian said, frustrated. "I had high hopes for you, boy! The both of you were supposed to be going to college and making something out of your lives. I wanted better for the both of you, and now you're fucking your lives up by bringing a child into this world."

"Wait a minute, Usian, you're being way too hard on them," Nika interjected. "Both of them graduated out of high school and still plan on going to college. They both have applied and gotten accepted to schools here in the city. CJ is going to go to UMSL, and Precious is going to go to nursing school after the baby is born."

"You seem to know a whole hell of a lot of their business," Usian uttered, annoyed.

"That's because we spend a lot of time together in the evenings, talking, when you're out there in the streets. If you weren't always running around with Whisper at night, you would be in on some of those conversations," Nika shot back.

Usian looked at her crossly because he was irritated that she was taking their side. "Look, we can continue this conversation later after I take them to the hospital."

"Would you like for me to go with you guys? I don't mind," Subira suggested. "I probably won't be able to go back to sleep anyway, because I'm going to be too concerned with Precious and the baby."

"That won't be necessary, Mama. I'm going to take them to the hospital," Usian spoke up. "Because all of them have some more explaining to do. I want to know how this was hidden under my nose, and I didn't see it, and my wife has some more explaining to do about keeping secrets."

Nika looked at her husband a bit shamefully as she headed toward the door. She knew it was a bad idea not to tell him, but it was too late to tell him now. In her heart, she felt like it was the right thing to do. She only hoped that Usian would eventually feel the same way.

Precious sat nervously on the bed, waiting for the doctor to come in and speak with her. She was hooked up to a blood pressure monitor and another machine that was keeping track of the baby's heartbeat. The doctor said it was a good sign that it was still strong, but that didn't make Precious feel any less worried. Also, to add to the stress, Usian was aware of the pregnancy, so her parents were sure to find out now. There was no way Precious would be able to go home once they were told, and CJ was still working on a place for them to live. Precious looked over at CJ, and the expression on his face was worse than the one she wore. How could they both be so irresponsible and not use protection? Only if Precious took her birth control pills like her mother instructed, all of this could have been avoided.

"Shit!" Precious called out. "I forgot my aunt works at this hospital. If she sees me here, I know she'll call my mother and tell them!"

"Calm down, Precious. You're making the baby's heart rate speed up, and I don't think that's good," CJ suggested calmly. "Does your aunt work in the ER?"

"No, but she works upstairs on the prenatal floor. She's one of the nurses who helps you deliver the baby," Precious explained. "If I have to stay in the hospital, I'm sure they're going to put me on that floor, and she'll see me for sure."

"You're worrying for nothing, Precious. Allah got us, and that's my word," CJ replied confidently. "If your aunt doesn't tell them, then Usian will definitely do it. I'm going to tell you something else. My uncle ain't going to trip with us really. He's going to go off on both of us and probably make you cry, but we're going to have to take that shit. He's not going to put me out, and when we tell him you can't go home, he'll help us find a place to stay for sure."

"You sound so confident, but sorry if I don't carry the same enthusiasm. Your uncle seems to hate me for some reason, and I don't understand why. Did you get that shit straight with him about the robbery?"

"If you mean telling him who robbed me, fuck naw... I really can't tell him the truth right now. I'm going to tell him eventually that Pooh robbed me," CJ said, sighing. "My uncle ain't going to trust me at all for real after all of this. The one thing he hates most in this world is a liar. He says that once a person lies to you, there's no way you could ever trust what they say after that."

"I hear you, nigga, but I need a fucking place to stay, and I can't live in that house if your uncle hates me!" Precious replied angrily. "You are such a fuck up sometimes, CJ, and this shit ain't cool, bruh. Is this the type of parent you're going to be to our child? Because if it is, I quit!"

Precious turned over on her side, nestling her head against her arm. She felt so defeated, and the pregnancy was well on its way. CJ needed to be a man and own up to his truth. Precious couldn't understand why CJ was so afraid of Usian knowing the truth about the robbery. However, if CJ didn't step up, then Precious was going to do it, and she didn't give a fuck if CJ got mad about it; at least he wouldn't be able to hit her.

"I promise I'm going to make shit right, baby," CJ whispered into her ear.

Precious readjusted her head so that CJ had to move his head. She didn't want to hear any of his bullshit promises right now, because they didn't mean anything. He was always promising shit that he couldn't deliver, and right now, this felt like all those other times.

"Why don't you let me be mad right now? Go see what Nika's doing in the waiting room," Precious suggested. "And I'm not asking."

"Okay, baby."

CJ placed a kiss on top of Precious's head and then on her shoulder. He grabbed the cover and pulled it up over her while Precious balled her body up. She was so scared for her baby and didn't know what to do. The stress and pressure of life was really getting to her.

CJ walked out into the waiting room and saw Nika sitting against the wall. She was staring out of the window, watching the traffic go down the street. CJ looked around the room for Usian, but he didn't see him.

"Hey, Nika, where's my uncle?" CJ asked curiously.

"He left," Nika replied softly. "He was pissed off that we kept this from him and didn't want to be around us right now."

"I'm sorry for dragging you in this."

"Are you?" Nika asked, looking up at him. "You were supposed to tell him last week. I don't give a fuck if you were waiting for the apartment; you promised me that you would tell him!"

"I know, Nika, and I'm sorry."

"Your sorry doesn't mean shit to me. My husband is quite upset with me and told me to get home the best fucking way I could. I didn't bring my purse with me since I left the house with him—that was dumb of me—so I don't have any money or cards with me to get home. I can't even buy myself anything to eat or drink."

Tears started running down her cheeks out of frustration. "I knew he would be mad, but I didn't expect this... I mean, how is his ass going to react if I really do something? Have you ever heard about your uncle hitting women?"

Nika stared at him like a deer in headlights. CJ didn't know how to respond, because he was already overwhelmed with thoughts. However, he knew that Usian would never do anything like that to her, because he didn't condone men hitting on women.

"You know my uncle loves you! There's no way he would hit you," CJ assured her. "He can be brutal sometimes with the way he handles situations, but it doesn't take long for him to get over stuff."

LATER THAT MORNING...

"Nika! Nika, wake up," Jabari said, shaking her vigorously.

He looked around the lobby, feeling annoyed. What the fuck was his best friend's wife doing sleep in the emergency room waiting area, and no one called to inform him that something was going on? Jabari shook Nika even harder one last time, causing her to jump up.

"Ahhh!" she yelled, looking discombobulated.

"Nika, it's me! It's Jabari."

She stared at him blankly for a second, trying to process her surroundings. "You're at BJC in the emergency room waiting area."

"Ah shit! I'm sorry, Jabari," Nika apologized. "What time is it?"

"It's almost ten in the morning. What are you doing here, and why didn't anyone call me? I've been here all night, doing a shift, and had no idea you were out here."

"I... well, CJ's girlfriend had a bit of a scare. She's pregnant and thought she was having a miscarriage, so we brought her to the hospital," Nika explained. "CJ was out here with me, but I guess he went back to check on his girlfriend."

"Where the fuck is Usian?" Jabari asked, confused.

"I don't know," Nika replied, rolling her eyes.

"Da fuck you mean, you don't know?"

Nika turned her nose up at Jabari and cocked her head to the side.

"Nigga, you heard what the fuck I said," Nika replied with an attitude. "He's pissed off on so many factors, Jabari. Usian had no idea that Precious was pregnant, but I knew. CJ made me promise not to say anything, because he wanted to tell Usian himself."

"And let me guess, he didn't tell Usian shit."

"He didn't tell Usian shit. We came home last night from our date, only to find my mother and aunt coming out of CJ's bedroom. It was late as fuck, and I know they were probably upstairs sleeping. My aunt said we needed to bring Precious to the hospital because it looked like she was miscarrying, and Usian flipped out."

"So how long did you know that she was pregnant?" Jabari asked nosily.

"I had only known for two weeks. CJ was supposed to tell Usian last week because that's what we agreed on. I should have known better than to keep this from Usian. I expected him to be angry with me over this shit, but it feels like he's taking it too far."

"Why would you agree to keep something like this from your husband? You guys aren't sneaking around anymore, and your position has changed in his life. He gave you his last name, and that shit means a lot! He needs to feel like he can trust you, but has your behavior given him any reason too?"

Nika looked at Jabari stupidly because she really didn't have a response. "On another note, I heard Jessica came over to y'all house drunk and got dusted off," Jabari teased.

A smirk appeared on Nika's face. "Good for you!"

"I could give a fuck less about that shit right now, Jabari; I don't mean no harm, but my husband is angry with me, and I need to figure out how to make it better."

"Did you drive to the hospital?" Jabari asked.

"Nope! The nigga left me sitting here and said my ass had to find a way home," Nika replied.

"He left you? You're bullshitting me!" Jabari said, getting loud. "He knows better than that!"

"It's all good. I was going to call my mama to come get me. I know she's up by now."

"How about I go check on Precious and CJ, then I'll drop you off at home," Jabari proposed.

"That's cool… if you don't mind," Nika said bashfully.

"Girl… I'll smack your ass! Quit playing with me," Jabari joked. "It's nothing, sis."

"Thank you, Jabari."

Jabari pushed Nika on the arm, causing her to fall over a little. She giggled and swung at him while Jabari moved away from her. He gave her a thumbs up and walked off toward the doors leading to the back. Nika laughed to herself as she reached into her pocket to grab her phone. She checked it and saw that Usian hadn't called or left a text message, so it was evident that he was still pissed at her. She wanted to desperately figure out a way to smooth things over before she made it home. Nika continued to rack her brain and was so distracted by her thoughts that she didn't see Roc walking up to her.

"What the fuck are you doing here!" Roc asked angrily. "I hope it's because someone fucked up that hoe ass nigga you snuck and married!"

Nika's eyes widened because she was taken back by his response.

"Nigga, fuck you! I don't owe you any explanation to why I'm here. Get the fuck out of my face, and go do something!" Nika spat angrily. "You wish a muthafucka fucked him up like he did you in the lobby of the Four Seasons."

"Bitch..." Roc replied, grabbing Nika by arm. "You better watch how the fuck you talk to me!"

He looked around the waiting room because he was in his scrubs, and the last thing he needed was for someone to see him manhandling Nika while he was at work. Roc had so much built-up anger toward Nika, and the one thing he would love to do was beat her ass up in this waiting room. "If we weren't in this waiting room, I would beat the shit out of you!"

"You ain't going to do shit to me, bitch ass nigga! You know my husband would kill you if touch me! You better hope he doesn't catch you after I tell him that you grabbed me," Nika replied, snatching away from him. "Now get the fuck on before he comes and catches you talking to me!"

Roc looked around nervously then back at Nika. He wasn't sure if Usian was there with Nika, but he didn't want to risk it. Besides, he needed to get upstairs to surgery since he was already five minutes late.

"You better be lucky that I'm running late," Roc said, sucking his teeth. "Bitch, don't let me catch you on the outside alone! 'Cause as God is my witness, I'm going to beat yo' ass!"

"You goin' do what?" CJ asked, pushing Roc from behind. "You got my auntie fucked up! We'll beat yo' ass up in here!"

"CJ, it's alright," Nika said, standing up.

The security guard stepped out of his room and looked down toward where they were. "Let his bitch ass go to work," Nika said. "But you're my witness when I tell my husband what the fuck he said."

"I ain't scared!" Roc declared. "Tell that nigga to come with it! He caught me by surprise the last time, but I'll fuck that nigga up if he steps to me again!"

"We gon' see," Nika said, chuckling. "Nigga, we gon' see!"

Ding... Ding... Ding... Ding... Boom! Boom! Boom! Boom!

"Wait, damn! Here I come!" Craig yelled.

Ding... Ding... Ding... Ding... Boom! Boom! Boom! Boom!

"I said wait a fucking minute!" Craig yelled louder.

He unlocked the door and swung it open aggressively.

"You have some nerve, showing your face around here!" Carlos said, putting his hands on his hips. "Because of you, shit is fucked up!"

"It ain't my fucking fault," Pooh replied, pushing past Carlos. "We didn't know that he was going to have an army securing his ass. Big Man jumped out to grab Usian, and out of nowhere, bullets started flying everywhere, and they weren't shooting little shit either!"

Carlos studied Pooh's walk as he hobbled over to the couch. He remembered Pooh telling him that he was shot, but Carlos thought it might have been a graze or something. Roc had called the hospital and talked to one of the nurses in the ER that liked him. She told him no one fitting Pooh's description came into the hospital. "Hurry up and shut that damn door! It's niggas out here looking for me!"

"Why are niggas looking for you? Didn't you have enough sense to cover your face? And I thought you said you got shot in the shoulder."

"I did get shot in the shoulder, but I got shot in the leg too. It doesn't mean shit if you cover your face. I've done so much shit in the past few months that a nigga always got to watch his back," Pooh explained. "You got some pain pills or something that I can take to help with this pain? The one bullet went straight through my shoulder, but there's still a bullet in my leg, and I need that one nigga to come take it out."

"Oh... so you're going to pretend like you don't know that nigga's name, and you sucked his dick?" Carlos asked, irritated.

"He fucked me too if you're keeping count, but that has nothing to do with you calling that nigga. I need for him to come take this shit out of my leg because I couldn't go to the hospital since a nigga is on parole," Pooh explained.

"I'm glad you didn't go to the police, because there's no telling what might have happened," Carlos said, walking over to his desk.

He pulled one of the drawers open and pulled out a large bottle of pills. "These are percs," Carlos said, handing him a handful of them. "I'll put a call into Roc, but what are you going to do for me?"

Pooh's brow furrowed as he glared at Carlos.

"What the fuck you mean? I'm sitting here shot, and all you can say to me is 'what can I do for you?' Bitch ass nigga, I wouldn't be shot if it wasn't for Roc's bitch ass! You better get that nigga on the phone before your ass be in the same predicament as I'm in," Pooh replied, whipping out his gun. "Now play with me if you want to!"

Carlos stood in place for a second, pissed off. He couldn't believe Pooh had pulled a gun out on him. He was merely joking with Pooh, but he had to take it too far.

"You know that's not necessary, don't you?" Carlos asked, rolling his eyes. "You young niggas kill me, always pulling out a gun. I bet you got your ass beat a lot as a kid. Were you this tough in the penitentiary?"

Carlos pulled his phone out of his pocket and dialed Roc's number. It went straight to voicemail, so he figured Roc was at the hospital. It would be a while before Roc checked his messages, but Carlos decided to leave one anyway. Pooh eyed Carlos crazily as he left a message.

"Why the fuck is you leaving a message?" Pooh asked angrily.

"Because Roc is at work, and he doesn't have his phone on while he's at the hospital," Carlos replied, feeling aggravated.

"I suggest your sweet ass call BJC and ask them to page his punk ass!" Pooh advised.

He grabbed a bottle of gin that was sitting on the table and took the cap off of it. He popped two of the pills into his mouth and washed it down with the drink. Carlos looked on, unamused, while Pooh downed the last of the alcohol in a few gulps. "You got something else to drink?" Pooh snapped.

"First of all, put that fucking gun down," Carlos snapped, folding his arms defensively. "Secondly, you're going to act like you have some manners and ask me like a grown ass man instead of a lil' punk bitch!"

A smirk appeared on Pooh's face, and he lowered the gun to his side. He loved the way Carlos came to him aggressively and decided to play along with his tough-guy act.

"I never pegged you for a tough guy," Pooh joked. "Can I get something else to drink… please?"

"That's more like it. Would you like dark or white?"

"I would like white. If you have some more gin, then that would be perfect," Pooh replied pleasantly.

"Let me go see what I have in the kitchen," Carlos said, putting the bottle of pills down on the table.

Carlos walked out of the room to go see what he had. He hoped to find some type of gin to give Pooh so that he could get drunk and pass out from the combination of pills and alcohol. Carlos didn't appreciate the way Pooh had come to him, especially the way he had fucked the entire kidnapping up. It was Pooh's fault that Usian hadn't gotten snatched up, but in retrospect, Nika was already married to Usian, so it wouldn't have made a difference anyway. However, they could have ransomed him off to her, and Roc still could have gotten the money owed to him.

Carlos grabbed a half of bottle of gin that was sitting on the counter and took it back out to Pooh. He wanted to put a teaspoon of rat poison in it, but that would only cause more problems. He handed it to Pooh and sat down on the couch next to him. Carlos noticed his bottle of pills had been hit, and only a small fraction of them were left. "You should have taken the whole damn bottle," Carlos hissed. "You can't leave shit around your bum ass. I bet you'd steal the sweetening off of sugar."

"What are you talking about?" Pooh asked, offended. "I ain't took shit!"

"You know what the fuck I'm talking about," Carlos replied dryly. "I'm not even going to entertain your bullshit, because you're full of shit." Carlos rolled his eyes at Pooh, and Pooh merely laughed at him.

"Thanks for the drink," Pooh said smugly. "And for your sake, you better hope Roc doesn't take too long to call back."

"I thought you didn't know his name, and here it is you've said it twice," Carlos said frankly. "How about we end this conversation so I can go back to watching television?"

"That's fine by me," Pooh replied with a bit of an attitude.

He opened the bottle of liquor and chugged down some of it. Carlos watched him through his peripheral vision, feeling disgusted while trying to concentrate on the television. How could he have ever messed with someone so sloppy? He thought Pooh was about that life because he talked so heavy. However, it was apparent that the only thing his ass was good for was stealing shit. Carlos even reached out to his friend Ed to get a reference for Pooh, and Ed gave him a stamp of approval. Usually, when Ed gave him a referral, the people he sent through were on the up and up. This nigga here was nothing but a character and might end up being a liability at the end of the day. Carlos had a lot to think about and would ponder over what to do with Pooh while he plowed deep inside of Pooh's asshole once he was intoxicated and couldn't resist.

CHAPTER

Eight

 $\mathcal{U}$sian was sitting at the lounge, having a drink. He had been there since happy hour started at five o'clock in the evening, and the evening regulars were drifting in for some late-night fun. He had been keeping Lay company the entire time, but when her husband Byrd came into the lounge, all of the attention went his way. Usian thought they were a cute couple, and they were the same age as Nika. The more he watched them interact with one another, he wondered if he came down too hard on her about the pregnancy situation.

Nika was only trying to do what was right, and he was sure she didn't want to be in the middle of CJ and Precious's shit. Usian spent the night at the braid shop because he didn't want to be around his wife. He had to process his feelings and emotions before sitting down and having a serious conversation with her. Nika had to learn that she didn't keep anything from him, no matter who it was trying to get her to do so. She broke one of the golden rules of marriage to him, and keeping secrets from one another was not going to be a regular practice. There were to be no secrets between them, no matter how hurtful they might be, because a marriage not built on trust would definitely fail.

"I knew I would find you here," Jabari said, sitting on the stool next to Usian.

"What you doing here? Aren't you supposed to be at the hospital?" Usian replied, taking a sip of his beer.

"I'm on break and decided to come find you so I can curse your stupid ass out," Jabari said, signaling Lay to come serve him.

"For what?" Usian asked, frowning.

"For leaving your wife in a hospital waiting room with no wallet or money to get home with," Jabari countered. "Her phone was on 20 percent when I found her sleep in one of the chairs at the hospital. Why would you leave her up there like that, bruh? That was hella stupid of you. Anything could have happened to Nika being left vulnerable like that."

Usian cut his eyes over at his friend and rolled them, unphased by his words. Usian didn't care what anyone thought, because Nika was his wife. He wanted to teach her a lesson, but a part of him felt a little crummy, and he didn't need Jabari coming around to make him feel any worse about his actions.

"Look, bruh, I know you're only looking out, but Nika's my bitch, and I don't need you to tell how to handle her. She was disobedient and needed to be punished for her actions."

"Do you hear yourself talking?" Jabari asked, disgusted. "You sound like the man you said you'll never be."

"What the fuck you mean by that?" Usian retorted back. "She kept something that was very important from me that I needed to know. It made me look stupid in front of Ms. Subira, and she's the last person I need to see that shit. Nika is supposed to tell me everything that she finds out or knows about a situation. I'm her husband, and she shouldn't keep shit from me. She made me look like a weak ass nigga in front of CJ. We're supposed to be a united front when it comes to that nigga. We talked about this at length before we got married. How is he going to respect my word if she's going behind my back, protecting him? And if that ain't enough for you, the little bitch Precious is pregnant, and I told you she stole that money from CJ."

"Yeah, I know all about the pregnancy. After I spoke with Nika—who, by the way, was in tears when she told me what happened, if you even care—I went upstairs to check on her, and the doctor wanted to keep her for observation, so I dropped Nika and CJ off at the house."

"CJ didn't stay up at the hospital?" Usian questioned.

"Nope," Jabari replied. "He said he had to go to work, and Precious understood that daddy needed to make shit happen."

Usian looked at Jabari in disbelief. "He really said that shit."

Both men started laughing. "I know you're upset with the lil' nigga, Usian, but at least he waited until he graduated high school to have a kid. Plus, he's going to college in the fall with a full-ride scholarship. Apparently, your bad ass nephew who skipped school still had enough sense to do his homework and have Precious turn it in to his teachers. Did you know that the only reason CJ didn't get honors was because of his attendance? That lil' nigga is smart as a muthafucka, and I think he's going to make something out of his life."

"But he's got a baby on the way. That nigga can't take care of himself, so how the fuck is he going to take care of a kid? All praises due to Allah that Precious has several little sisters and brothers that she's helped raised because CJ don't know shit! And for the record, I knew that my nephew was smart. He could have been valedictorian if his attendance wasn't fucked up."

"And that's okay," Jabari rebutted. "He'll learn how to take care of his seed. That's why it's important that he has a strong support system. You and Nika will help guide your oldest boy on the right path."

Usian's eyes widened while Jabari looked at him and laughed. "Don't look at me like that, nigga. This shit you're going through right now is a rehearsal for what you're going to go through when Nika has a baby. Your child is going to give you the fucking blues like you did your mama. Speaking of which, here's your mama coming through the door right now," Jabari said, pointing.

Jackie and a couple of her friends walked through the front entrance. She spotted Usian sitting over at his usual spot and stared evilly at him. She pointed her finger in his direction and headed straight toward him.

"Shit! Here she comes," Usian said, moaning.

"Can you tell me why you're not answering the phone for your wife?" Jackie demanded. "I was sitting on the porch with Subira when Nika walked up. I asked her to call you, and she said you weren't taking any of her calls. I asked her why, and she went on to tell me that Precious's big-headed ass was pregnant, and you were mad at her because she didn't tell you. Now, if that ain't some stupid shit! You could be mad at her, but damn, Usian... Leaving her at the hospital and not taking her phone calls is a bit extreme."

"I tried to talk to him, Mama, but the nigga doesn't want to listen," Jabari added. "Nika is so sorry for not telling you that she's almost on the verge of a panic attack."

"I think Jabari's ass is exaggerating, but it's not sitting right with her, son. She smoked at least two blunts while we were out there talking, and I was there for about an hour and a half," Jackie recalled. "You're stressing that poor girl out before she can even conceive my grandchild. I'm going to whoop your ass, Usian, if that girl doesn't get pregnant!"

"Mama, I'm not stressing Nika out!" Usian protested. "I'll admit that I've overreacted about the CJ situation, but you're going a bit too far, saying I'm not going to get my wife pregnant."

Some of the people around them were chuckling and laughing at Usian and his mother's conversation. There was a couple sitting at the bar who started to have a conversation about the situation. Usian noticed that people were homed in on them, and he didn't like it. He stared at all of them with a mean grimace on his face and stopped when he noticed Nika coming into the lounge.

She had on a pair of wide-legged, pink cotton pants with a tight-fitting, white, swoop-neck T-shirt. Her breasts were sitting up high like he liked them, and her pants hugged her ass just right but not to the point where they looked nasty. He told Nika it was all right for her to dress sexy, but he would prefer for it to be done modestly. He even told her that it was her choice if she wanted to wear a hijab every day. The only time he asked that she wore it was during prayer and when they went to the temple. Nika had no problem granting these small requests for her husband, and she even kept her hair braided in cute styles because Usian loved them on her. She currently had her hair two stranded with some of them pulled up in a ponytail. She wore some gold embellishment sporadically throughout the twist that set them off. Usian loved looking at his beautiful, chocolate wife and needed to make things right with her.

"I figured I would find you here," Nika said, walking up to him.

"Give your husband a kiss," Usian demanded.

"I wouldn't give him shit!" Jackie said, frowning.

Usian glared over at his mother while Nika and Jabari chuckled. "You see I'm not laughing because I'm deadass serious."

Nika walked closer and gave her husband a peck on the lips. Usian ceased her in his arms and planted a passionate yet tender kiss on her lips. Nika melted into his arms, and Jackie rolled her eyes at the sight.

"That nigga's got magical powers over her, Mama. You might as well say he's got the R. Kelly effect!" Jabari joked.

"You got me fucked up!" Usian said, breaking away from Nika. "My wife is of legal age, nigga! I don't care if I am several years older than her. Nika will be twenty-five soon, and her mother will back me up on that!"

Everyone started laughing, and Usian kissed Nika again quickly. "I'm sorry for being such an asshole to you," Usian whispered in Nika's ear. "I love you."

He planted one more kiss against her temple and hugged her tightly.

"Don't forgive that nigga so quickly," Jackie protested. "Make his ass sweat it out, and don't give him no pussy tonight!"

"Okay, Mama, it's time for you to go find your friends," Usian said, breaking away from Nika.

He pushed his mother toward the aisle, and she laughed, swatting at him. He wrapped his arms around his mother, squeezing her tight. He told her he loved her, kissed her on the forehead, and sent her to her friends. "Aye, Lay, I got my mama and her friends," he called out.

"Okay, Usian," Lay replied, giving him the thumbs up.

Usian made his way back over to Nika and collected her into his arms. He hugged her tightly and buried his face in the nape of her neck. He breathed in her familiar scent, and his joint instantly rose. Nika giggled against his chest because she felt her best friend lurking. She was horny for her husband from the way he treated her when she arrived at the lounge. It seemed like she was always horny for Usian, and she wondered if this feeling was ever going to end.

"I take it you missed me even though you were being an asshole," Nika said sarcastically.

Usian pulled away a little bit and stared down at her. "Those were your words, sir."

"They were, in fact, my words, and I will accept them. I really am sorry for how I flew off the handle at you," Usian apologized. "I guess I was so frustrated that it came out of anger."

"Don't believe nothing that nigga says, sis! He's full of shit!" Jabari teased.

"Shouldn't you be headed back to the hospital?" Usian questioned smugly.

Jabari looked down at his watch. "Indeed, I do, bruh," Jabari replied, standing. "I'll catch the two of you later... Better yet, we're having dinner together on Thursday."

"Why Thursday, bruh?" Usian asked curiously.

"Because that's my day off," Jabari replied.

"Sounds good to me," Nika added. "I'll cook dinner."

"Sounds like a plan," Jabari confirmed. "Love you both!"

"Love you too!" the couple replied in unison.

They looked at each other and laughed. Usian quickly kissed her lips and squeezed two handfuls of her ass. His joint thumped against his leg, and Nika smiled wickedly at him because she felt it too. Her insides were so wet that there should've been a stain in the seat of her pants. Usian looked around for a second before grabbing Nika's hand and taking off toward the back of the lounge. He was about to introduce Nika to one of the many secret spots at his favorite place.

Usian took Nika to the apartment attached to the lounge. He pushed the door closed behind him and aggressively grabbed Nika from behind. He pressed his erection into the crease of her butt while he reached his hands up under her shirt. He pinched her nipples and kissed her neck while Nika rolled against him. She grabbed the waist of her pants and pulled them down, exposing her thong. Usian damn near had a fit when he saw it and dropped to his knees. He bent Nika over and buried his face in between her legs. He used his finger to move her thong to the side and shoved his tongue deep inside of her folds. Nika moaned as she shook her goodness in his face.

Usian greedily ate her pussy, licking and sucking all of the juices that were escaping from her honey pot. He pushed two fingers inside of Nika's super tight walls, and his hand was damn near covered from her wetness. He latched on to her clit and sucked in hard. He beat his tongue against it, and Nika's legs buckled from the pressure. Usian cupped her butt with his free hand and pushed her back up to her feet. He came from up under her and stood to his feet. He swooped her up, threw her over his shoulder, and took her into one of the bedrooms in the front of the apartment.

Nika was nervous because she had never been to this particular part of

VIVIAN BLUE

the lounge. Usian often told her about the other rooms and the apartment, but she had never been in any of them. Usian slapped Nika on the ass and dropped her on the bed. He took the sandals she was wearing off her feet before grabbing the bottom of her pants and taking them the rest of the way off. Next, he grabbed the waist of her thong and took them off too. His dick was about to jump out of his basketball shorts, so he urgently removed them and his underwear. Nika instantly got on all fours and climbed over to him. She gripped his joint with one hand and swirled her tongue around the head of it. She deep throated him two times, gagging on her way back up, but as much as Usian loved for his wife to give him head, all he wanted was some of her tight twat. Usian slid his dick out of Nika's mouth, and she frowned at him disapprovingly.

"Lay back, baby," Usian instructed. "That shit felt good, but I want to put my dick in some of this good pussy."

Nika did as she was told and lay on her back. Usian grabbed her by the leg and pulled her almost to the edge of the bed. He climbed on the bed and dug his knees into the mattress, gripping the edge of it with his feet. He placed Nika's legs on his shoulders and kissed up and down her calf while he rubbed the head of his erection against her sopping wet folds. Nika shuttered at the feeling and pushed forward slightly, inserting the head of his dick inside of her. A slight smile appeared on Usian's face because his lil' baby was horny as a muthafucka.

He pushed his long, thick rod deep inside of Nika, and she let out a throaty moan as she eased back some. Usian put his hands on her hips and pulled her back down on his stiffness. He could tell it was uncomfortable for his baby, but she was going to be all right in a minute. He worked her pussy at a slow but steady pace, making Nika go absolutely crazy. He could hear her juices making sloshing noising, and it farted a few times when he pushed deep, deep down inside of her womb. He was enjoying the feel of her tightness, but Usian really needed to nut.

"I'm about to quit playing with you, baby," Usian said, leaning down and kissing her lips. "I'm about to knock the dust out of this pussy and make you nut so hard that you're going to feel it on the car ride home."

"You talk so muuuuu—" Nika's words got caught in her throat when Usian began to serve her a proper dick down.

He was plowing her walls hard and fast, not showing any mercy. Nika grabbed a hold of his wrist, trying to brace herself, but the way he was assaulting her pussy, it really didn't matter. Usian and Nika's eyes were locked on to each other until he knocked deep down inside of her. Nika's eyes rolled in the back of her head, and for a moment, Usian thought she was possessed. He licked two of his fingers then played with Nika's clit. He had her so wired up that her orgasm exploded through her body. She let out a scream of satisfaction that was heard all through the bar. Big Lee was behind the bar and rang the bell because she knew exactly what was going on. Lay told her mother that Usian was a bit drunk, and Big Lee knew that he and Nika had gotten into an argument last night. Lay went on to say that Usian took his wife in the back to the apartment, so Big Lee knew that it was some makeup sex going on.

"Got damn, bae!" Nika yelled, gripping the comforter. "Ooooooo... fuck yeah! Fuck yeah, baby!"

Usian continued to hammer her pussy because he had yet to nut. It was feeling so good to him that he kept holding out, but this time, it was coming so powerfully that he couldn't do anything but release. He pumped hard and deep inside Nika then sank all the way down into her folds.

"Fuuuuuuuuuuuucccccckkkkkkk!" Usian shouted, nutting deeply inside of her.

His body was dripping with sweat, and Nika's shirt was trashed. "I love your funky ass!" Usian said, smiling. He leaned forward and kissed her passionately. "I love you so much, baby."

"I love you too," Nika replied, giggling.

They held each other for a while before getting up to take a quick shower. Usian couldn't resist himself, and they did it again in the showers. By the time they left the lounge, it was closed, and Whisper had to come back to let them out.

CHAPTER

Nika and CJ were up early the next morning. They were sitting in the kitchen, discussing Precious and what was going to happen next. She was getting released from the hospital today, and her mother made it perfectly clear that she couldn't come home. CJ was depressed because he didn't know what to do. Nika had made him a big stack of pancakes, chicken sausages, scrambled eggs with cheese, smothered potatoes, and grits, trying to cheer him up. CJ was overwhelmed with the amount of food Nika had put on his plate. He wondered what had gotten into her, but he smelled remnants of her favorite herbal spice in the air and figured it must have motivated her to cook all of this food. It wasn't until he saw Usian that he realized what was going on with his auntie.

Usian walked into the kitchen and went straight over to Nika. He put his hand on her butt and gripped it, planting a kiss on the nape of her neck. Nika leaned her head over to the side, exposing more of it. Usian took advantage of it and bit down like a vampire.

"Good morning, Mrs. Simpson," Usian said, hugging her body.

"Good morning, Mr. Simpson," Nika replied, giggling.

Usian slapped her on the ass and walked over to the refrigerator. He grabbed a bottle of water then went over to the table to sit down. CJ felt both nervous and anxious when Usian sat down, so he grabbed his plate and got up from the table. "Aren't you going to finish your breakfast?" Nika asked, staring at him.

"I was going to give y'all some privacy and go eat in my room," CJ replied.

"You will sit at the table and eat with us like you normally do," Usian said sternly. "Besides, we need to discuss this Precious situation, and you're going to be completely honest with me. This is your one time to clear the slate, so be wise in what you decide to tell me and what you decide to keep to yourself."

Nika put Usian's plate down in front of him and kissed his lips softly. She gazed down at him, smiling warmly before returning over to the stove. She brought a smaller saucer with two pieces of toast on it and set it down next to the other plate. Nika was on cloud nine after last night's and this morning's make-up sex they had. They started at the lounge, had a round in the backseat of her car, and managed to make it to the porch before having sex in the doorway. Nika went to take a shower once they walked inside of the house, but Usian came to join her, and it was on and popping again. Once they took care of their hygiene, they went and got in the bed where Usian couldn't control himself, and they were back at it again until they fell asleep in each other's arms.

"Do you need anything else, my king?" Nika asked lovingly.

"Can you get me the apple jelly, please?" Usian asked politely.

"I sure can," Nika replied, smiling wide.

She switched her hips over to the refrigerator, opening the door swiftly. She grabbed the jelly and took it over to him. She placed it on the table then gave her husband one last kiss before she went over to the sink to wash the dishes. Nika grabbed her wireless earbuds off the counter and placed them in her ears. She started singing and swaying to the music while Usian fixed his food and swayed his head to the music. He had a smile on his face and was mouthing the words to the song Nika was singing. Lauren Hill and D'Angelo's "Nothing Really Matters" had the couple in sync, and CJ stared at them in disbelief.

"What's the matter with you?" Usian asked, taking a bite of his eggs.

"Nothing's wrong with me," CJ replied defensively. "What's wrong with Nika?"

Usian looked over at his wife and smiled at her singing and dancing.

"Whatever it takes to make you happy, baby. Whatever it takes to make you smile. Whatever it takes to make you feel good, baby, I'll be around," Nika sang. She loved Anita Baker and knew almost every song she put out. Her mother used to listen to that particular song on repeat for hours when she was thinking about her late husband. Subira would clutch the picture to her chest and cry her eyes out while Nika held her mother in her arms and wiped away the tears.

"I'd make you feel like never before. Here I stand, heart in hand. Help me find the door. Anybody can see, baby, you've been hurt before. Let me heal your pain. Won't ever hurt no more..."

"Nika must be feeling those words," CJ uttered, chuckling. "She's singing the mess out of those words."

Usian didn't respond and continued to eat his food. "Unc, I'm sorry about not telling you about Precious being pregnant. I was trying to be a man and handle my business," CJ explained.

"I understand, CJ, but you still should have been a man and came to talk to me. I'm glad that you've graduated out of high school, but you still have a whole future ahead of you," Usian replied, putting his fork down on the plate.

He paused for a second, staring at Nika. She was breaking it down at the sink, and it seemed to have distracted Usian. CJ turned around to see what Usian was looking at and laughed at his uncle's response to his wife. He could tell that Usian was so much in love with his wife, and CJ hoped that he would feel the same way about Precious when they got married. "You see your aunt over there dancing and shit? She's happy than a muthafucka, and you want to know why? Because I knocked the bottom out of that pussy last night and this morning," Usian bragged, taking a bite out of his sausage. "I'm getting hard, sitting here, watching her bounce that ass over at the sink!"

"That's too much information, Unc," CJ replied, eating his food. "Nika's been walking around the kitchen this morning like she's floating on a cloud."

"She is floating on a cloud, nigga! She's floating on a dick cloud that I put her ass on," Usian joked.

"I heard that!" Nika said, glancing over her shoulder.

"So! It ain't like I whispered the shit or something. You know your ass is doped up off this dick, and I'm about to give your ass some more once

I'm done eating this big ass breakfast you made. You gave me toast and pancakes, baby, so I know I handled you proper," Usian boasted.

"You did put your work in, daddy, but I'm not fucking around with you this morning. I have a client in an hour, and I can't be late, fucking around with you," Nika replied.

"I guess I need to stop eating so we can go handle some business," Usian suggested.

"I think you better sit there and eat your food before it gets cold, and maybe mama can knock you off before I leave," Nika said, headed toward the door. "And don't forget to have your talk with CJ. Precious has to be picked up from the hospital by noon."

She walked out of the room, and Usian watched her disappear. A smirk came over his face, and he laughed as he put some food in his mouth.

"She's walking a little bow-legged," Usian uttered, chuckling to himself. "Boy, I'm telling you that I'm so in love with that woman. I'll kill a muthafucka with my bare hands if they fuck with her."

"Did Nika tell you about what happened in the hospital when Roc saw her?" CJ asked.

"Yeah, she told me, and I'm going to beat his ass again when I see him. Death would be too great for the nigga, and I want him to be tortured every time he sees me or my wife," Usian stated frankly. "He thinks he can intimidate Nika, but I'm going to let his bitch ass know once and for all that I'm not playing with him."

"Can I ask you a question?"

"Sure, CJ. Shoot."

"Can Precious come here to live with us?" CJ asked, holding his head down.

Usian didn't like the way his nephew cowered when it came to speaking with him. He was glad that CJ feared him, but he didn't want his nephew to be afraid to tell him anything. CJ needed to know that Usian loved and cared about him; that was why he's always so hard on him.

"CJ, hold your damn head up, and look me in the eye when you're speaking to me. You're a man now who's about to have a kid!" Usian fussed. "And you better look every muthafucka you come in contact with in the eye when you're talking to them! I noticed you talk real greasy to

Precious, but you cower when it's time to stand up to a man, and that's some bullshit!"

"I don't—"

"You's a lie, and the truth ain't in you," Usian said, cutting him off. "Nika told me about a conversation she had with Precious. Precious thinks I hate her because you lied about the robbery. You put it on her when that little weak ass nigga Pooh was the one who robbed you."

CJ looked up at him like he'd seen a ghost. "Yeah, nigga… I know the truth. Why didn't you tell me that Pooh was the one who done it? I would have taken care of that shit ASAP!"

"Because I wanted to take care of it myself," CJ replied. "I can't live in your shadow, Usian, and always count on you to handle my beefs. I was going to handle that nigga, but I was distracted by Precious being pregnant and you gaining a wife."

Usian studied his nephew for a minute and thought about his words. He was happy that CJ was finally being honest with him, but he realized there was a lot of growing up that CJ still needed to do. Usian felt like he was failing at teaching him to be a man because he was too busy teaching CJ how to be a hustler. "It ain't easy, being your nephew and working for your best friend. I get tired of hearing about what you did back in the day, how you move out in the streets now, and how I'm nothing like you."

"I don't expect you to be like me, CJ. I expect you to be better," Usian replied sincerely. "I don't want you to make the same mistakes I made. You're better than this street life, and I'm trying my best to protect you from the real horrors of being a drug dealer. Do you know what I would have done to you if you weren't my nephew and came up short? I've killed niggas for less than that, and this is the life that you want for yourself?"

"Yes… I mean, no… I mean… I don't know," CJ uttered. "I just want to make a shit load of money so that my girl and my seed don't have to want for shit."

"And you can have that if you get a college degree. You're smart enough to start your own business and thrive. I've been talking to Big Lee about how you're good at computers, and she's thinking about having you come work for her in the office. I'm not saying that you're not cut out for the streets, but I refuse to lose you like I've lost my brother and your mother. I made a promise to your mama that you're going to make something out of your life, and you're going to do it whether I have to beat your ass until you get it or you get it on your own. I love you, CJ, and I will never abandon you or turn my back on you."

"I love you too, Unc," CJ replied, feeling emotional. "You're all I got, and if you would have—"

"Don't even speak on it," Usian replied firmly. "I didn't, and I'm not... That's all that's important, understand?"

"Yes, sir."

"Now, if you'll excuse me," Usian said. "I have to go get a quickie in before my wife leaves for work."

Usian got up from his chair and walked off to find Nika. CJ let out a sigh of relief before laughing at his uncle. He was happy that they had this conversation, and CJ had a better understanding of where Usian was coming from. His uncle truly loved him unconditionally, and CJ hoped he could grow to be the type of man Usian wanted him to be.

Usian had dropped CJ off at the front doors of BJC so he could go get Precious. He didn't feel like going inside and waiting, so he decided to sit outside in the truck. He fired up a blunt and called back Whisper to talk about where he could take Nika for dinner, but it soon went on a dialogue about the nigga Pooh. Word on the street was that Pooh was hired by some nigga from Chicago to kidnap Usian. Usian didn't understand why someone from Chicago would want to kidnap him, but he did fuck a dude up in prison from the Chi.

He was watching the traffic and just so happened to turn his head. He spotted Roc coming out of the hospital garage and decided to follow him. He had a bone to pick with him about Nika, and now was as good a time as any to address it. Usian told Whisper he'd call him back and put his truck in drive.

Roc made a right at the light and headed down Kingshighway Boulevard. Usian called CJ and told him that he was making a run and would be back in twenty minutes. Usian wasn't sure where Roc was headed, but he would pull up on him and yank his ass out of the car if they went too far away from the hospital. Roc made a right onto the Forrest Park Expressway, so Usian did the same. He followed Roc down to Newstead Avenue and figured that Roc was going to the gas station when they made a left turn. Roc pulled up on the lot and hopped out of the car with it still running. Usian pulled up on the lot at the pump right across from him and got out of his truck. He went and leaned on Roc's car in plain view so that he would be seen when Roc came out of the door.

"Mister, there's someone leaning against your car," the gas station attendant mentioned.

Roc looked out the window and spotted Usian. "Would you like for me to call the police?"

"That won't be ne—Yes, call the police," Roc said, putting his money into the slot. "I'm sure he's not a threat, but I can't be too sure."

The attendant called the police while he bagged Roc's items. Roc was nervous as hell, but he tried to pretend like he wasn't. He slowly walked out of the door of the gas station and headed over to his car.

"What the fuck you leaning on my car for?" Roc hissed.

"Why the fuck are you talking to my wife like you're crazy or something?" Usian shot back, standing straight up. "I told you not to say shit to Nika, and I thought I made myself perfectly clear when I beat your ass in the lobby of the hotel."

"You got some lucky shit off, and I guess you think you're tough, big man," Roc replied. "I'm not scared of you, Usian, and that cunt of a wife of yours owes me money!"

Roc saw the police coming down the street, so he felt brave enough to talk shit to Usian. He knew that Usian had a record and did some time in a federal penitentiary, so Roc figured the last thing Usian wanted was to be arrested. "You hit the jackpot and thought that I was going to go away quietly. Well, I got news for you; that bitch is going to pay me royally!"

Usian didn't say a word and stared at Roc nonchalantly. He reached back and punched Roc square in the face, and Roc hit the ground like deadweight. The police car pulled up on the lot and hit their lights. Usian looked back at them and smirked. He figured he was going to jail, but this was well worth it. He'd call Whisper to come bail him out then go looking for Roc to finish what he'd started.

CHAPTER

*P*recious looked out the door as her brother pulled up a few doors down from CJ's house after Usian questioned him about Pooh's whereabouts. He was petrified of the dude. He lied and told his parents that he'd been robbed by a group of men when he came out of a club. Trey didn't want to tell on Pooh, because he would be signing his own death wish. Precious walked out of the house and signaled for him to get out of the car, but Trey waved her to come to him. Precious rolled her eyes in her head as she walked out of the gate and headed to her brother.

It was hot and humid as muthafucka, and it felt like her skin was melting off her body. She didn't understand why he was being so secretive, but it didn't matter, because she wanted to get out of the house anyway. Ever since she had that miscarriage scare, the doctor had put her on bed rest for the next two weeks. It had only been a few hours, and CJ was already getting on her nerves. Precious was so happy that he had to go to work that she gave him a blow job before he left. What she didn't expect was for him to ask Ms. Subira to keep an eye on her, but she was so cool that Precious didn't mind.

"Why you got me walking all the way down here to your car?" Precious complained. "I'm supposed to be on two weeks bed rest, and it's hot as lil' sis puss out here."

"Stop your complaining and get in the car. I got the AC on," Trey said, checking his rearview mirror. "Where's your man at?"

Trey hit his cigarette two more times before throwing it out of the window.

"He's gone to work," Precious replied, getting in the car. "I don't know why you're so scared to come up to the house. I thought you and CJ were cool."

"We are cool, but I don't know how his uncle Usian is going to feel about me being on his front."

Precious gave him a crazy look. "Don't look at me like that. You know his uncle sells big dope, and he doesn't play with people," Trey said, looking around. "If I tell you something, you have to promise not to say anything to anyone."

"Who am I going to tell, Trey? I don't have no friends."

"You got a punk ass baby daddy, and I'm sure you'll run your mouth to him," Trey replied, sounding frustrated. "You know Mama and Daddy are pissed at you."

"I know," Precious replied, rolling her eyes. "Mama told me to come get my shit off the porch because I can't come there. I can't believe she's that upset with me. I've graduated from high school. What more does she want for me?"

"She wanted your stupid ass to be better than she was at your age. Mama started having kids at sixteen and continued to push you mutha-fuckas out continuously after that until she got her tubes tied."

"I'm not like her, Trey. I'm not having eight kids!" Precious insisted. "This little baby growing inside of me isn't going to stop me from making something out of my life. I'm going to nursing school after I have this baby, and Nika, Usian's wife, is going to teach me how to braid hair so I can work in her shop. I'll be able to do it up until I have the baby, and she said once the doctor clears me, she'll let me come back to the shop."

"It sounds like you've got it all figured out," Trey said, smiling at his sister. "What is that nigga CJ doing? It sounds like his family is the one doing everything."

"CJ is being a very responsible adult. He's trying to secure us an apartment even though his uncle wants us to remain in his house. He said that we're going to need a lot of support once the baby comes, but I beg to differ. He and his wife are newlyweds, and all it seems like they do is fuck," Precious said, sucking her teeth. "I thought me and CJ got it in, but those two are ridiculous!"

"Ah, yeah," Trey said, laughing.

"Yes!" Precious validated. "Nika was a virgin when they got married. She was supposed to be marrying this dude named Roc, but Usian slid in and snatched her right up from under his nose. I argued with CJ so many times that Nika wasn't a virgin, the way she and Usian used to be all up in each other's face, but CJ swore on his father's grave that Nika was a virgin. She even told me that she was a virgin up until their wedding night."

"You said she was supposed to marry a dude named Roc. Is he from Chicago?"

"I don't know where the hell he's from, but I know he works at the hospital. CJ said something about he's studying to be a surgeon," Precious explained. "I don't know how she picked Usian over a surgeon, but I guess she knows something that I don't."

Precious hunched her shoulders and slumped down into the seat.

"Girl, yo' ass is stupid. I would have picked Usian's ass too over a surgeon," Trey said, shaking his head. "Usian is out here getting money. He's a made man on these streets, and he's the righthand man of Whisper. Whisper is married to Big Lee, and you know she's the queen pin of the city."

"Well, if Usian got all of this money, why is it that he's living in a two-family flat, paying rent to Ms. Subira?" Precious asked sarcastically. "I mean, he dresses nicely and has damn near every tennis shoe ever made stacked up on shelves in the basement. His jewelry is fresh, and Nika is always laced in designer, but that shit is ghetto rich shit—stuff people do in order to floss for their friends."

"Your ass is dumb," Trey replied, shaking his head again. "That's all a front. I happen to know for a fact that Usian is getting paid; that's why Pooh wanted to snatch him up."

"What you mean, Pooh wanted to snatch him up?" Precious stared at her brother with her brow furrowed. "You better start talking, Trey, since you've already opened your mouth."

Trey let out a deep breath and leaned his head against the back of the seat. He didn't want to tell Precious about what he knew, but he'd already opened his big mouth. He was about to tell her earlier but changed the subject instead since he could be killed for telling what he knew. "Cat got your tongue, nigga? Spit it out!" Precious demanded.

"Okay, damn, Precious!" Trey uttered, annoyed. "Pooh reached out to me the other day, saying that he had a lick for me. He couldn't go into much detail with me, because we were on the phone, but he said it had something to do with Usian."

"Whaaaaatttt?" Precious exclaimed in shock. "Now you know that's fucked up!"

"Yeah... now, shut the fuck up before someone hears you!" Trey demanded. "I haven't finished telling you everything."

"Well, hurry the fuck up then because I want to know all the tea," Precious replied, turning up her lips.

She knew she promised her brother she wouldn't say anything, but there was no way she was going to keep this from CJ. She listened to Usian talk to Nika about trust, and if she and CJ were going to make it, there was no way she was going to keep this type of information from him. "Do you know if someone is putting him up to this?"

"I don't know," Trey replied, firing up a cigarette.

Precious waved her hand in front of her face in a dramatic manner. Trey watched and rolled his eyes while he let down the window. He knew that he'd told Precious too much, and she was probably going to tell CJ what he'd said. "Don't go shooting your mouth off to CJ, you hear me?" Trey asked, blowing smoke out of the window. "I could lose my life by telling you about it."

"I don't see why your stupid ass keeps associating with Pooh. I bet he's the reason why you got your ass beat... ain't he?" Precious questioned. "CJ told me that Pooh was a fag. Are the two of you fucking around?"

"Bitch, what?" Trey uttered. "Girl, I'll beat your ass!"

"And I'll beat yours," CJ said, standing outside of Trey's window.

He leaned down and peered into the car.

"What the fuck you doing out here? Didn't the doctor say you had to stay in the bed for two weeks?" CJ asked sternly. "And get the fuck out of the car! Why are you sitting in there, and he's smoking a cigarette? You must be trying to kill my seed!"

"It's hot outside, and I'm sitting in an air-conditioned car. It feels good in here, and the window's down," Precious pointed out.

"Shut yo' crybaby ass up, nigga," Trey joked, chuckling.

"Aye... fuck you," CJ replied. "Just because yo' infertile ass can't have kids don't mean you're going to kill mine!"

They both laughed. Precious got out of the car and walked around to the sidewalk. She went and stood next to CJ, and he put his arm around her shoulders. She looked up at him with a half-smile on her face, so he kissed her lips softly and sucked on the bottom one.

"For the record, I got a daughter, nigga... and don't be doing that shit in front of me!" Trey complained. "That's what got yo' ass put out in the first place."

"Fuck you, Trey!" Precious shot back.

"Speaking of which, I forgot to tell you that I got your shit in the trunk of my car. Ma put your stuff on the porch, and I didn't want anyone to come by and steal it. She put it all in trash bags, but everyone knows that you got some dope shit, so they would have raided those bags in a heart-beat," Trey explained. "CJ, why don't you help her take the shit in the house?"

"How about you get your bitch ass out and help me take her shit in the house," CJ fussed. "She's pregnant and can't lift shit. Didn't she tell you she almost had a miscarriage?"

"I thought she was just talking shit. My fault, sis... I didn't know," Trey said, getting out the car. "I don't care that you're pregnant. I can't wait to meet my nephew."

"Don't you start that shit too! CJ seems to think for some reason that I'm having a boy, but I think it's going to be a girl. Ms. Subira said that we won't be able to tell until I get bigger," Precious explained. "She's going to deliver the baby here at the house. She and Zaida were midwives in Africa in their village. They even delivered some of their friends' kids and their kids here in the states."

She sounded so excited, and Trey could see she was happy. He felt bad about all of the dumb shit that he'd been a part of with Pooh. If Trey wanted to have a relationship with his sister's kid, then he needed to come clean with her man. Trey didn't know how CJ was going to take what he had to say, but at least he was manning up to tell him.

⁓ "C'mon so we can take this shit in the house and smoke a blunt," CJ said, walking toward the trunk.

"I'm sitting in the car with y'all so I can get high off contact," Precious said, rubbing her stomach.

She wasn't showing at all, but her stomach was starting to get hard.

"Bi…" CJ uttered, looking at her angrily. "I mean thot! Yo' ass ain't about to be sitting in no car with us while we smoke weed! Are you stupid or something?"

"I'm telling Usian that you called me a thot!" Precious hissed, stomping her foot. "You promised him that you would talk to me with respect!"

"Girl, you know I was just playing," CJ teased. "Sorry, not sorry…"

He hunched his shoulders, making Precious even angrier. She stormed off toward the house, and Trey laughed as he pulled out one of the trash bags filled with clothes out of the trunk. "Baby! Can you at least stand there and hold the screen door?" CJ begged.

"Y'all ass is crazy, bruh!" Trey said, handing off the bag to CJ. "Aye… I want to holla at you once we're done. I need to rap with you about something."

"Alright, nigga," CJ replied, slinging the bag over his shoulder. "Let's hurry the fuck up because it's hot as fuck out here."

"I'm right behind you, bruh."

CJ and Trey managed to get all of the bags out of the trunk and into the house. Precious had so much stuff that Ms. Subira suggested that CJ go to the store to buy containers. He was happy to go since there wasn't anywhere for him to sit. Plus, he desperately wanted to smoke a blunt because he found out that he was denied the apartment.

"What did you want to talk to me about?" CJ asked, passing Trey a blunt.

"I uhhh… I wanted to tell yo' punk ass that you better take care of my lil' sister and treat her right. I know you be putting your hands on her, but I'm going to kick your ass if she ever tells me you hit her for real!" Trey threatened.

He hit the blunt and coughed, making CJ laugh at him.

"That's what the fuck you get for talking shit," CJ replied. "But for real, what did you want to talk to me about?"

Trey hit the blunt again and held the smoke. He French cut it through his nostrils to his mouth and studied CJ for a second. He blew out the smoke and took one more hit then passed it off to CJ.

"I don't know how to say this, so I'm just going to spit it out. Pooh was the one who killed your mama. He threatened to kill Precious if I told you and then said he would kill me after my mama buried her," Trey confessed nervously. "I'm sorry that I got you involved with that dude, but I had nothing to do with your mother's death."

"I know," CJ replied softly. "I was on the porch and saw him drive past in the same car he had stolen a few days prior. I know he was trying to hit me, but my mama was in the way."

"That nigga is fucked up in the head," Trey said, reaching for the blunt.

"I know, but I'm going to kill that nigga for all the shit he's done to me," CJ replied seriously. "I've been looking for his ass, but the nigga seems to have vanished in thin air."

"I might be able to flush his ass out. Give me a few days, and I'll hit you up with something," Trey promised. "In the meantime, you treat my little sister right, and make sure she doesn't bury you in shoes, purses, and clothing!"

"Bet. That nigga needs to be taken up off this muthafucka, and I plan on being the one to do it," CJ uttered. "And I put that on my mama!"

CHAPTER

*B*araka rushed into the emergency room doors, trying to find his son. He had gotten a call from his wife, stating that she'd gotten a call from the hospital that Roc had been brought in by the ambulance. He didn't have a clear story of what happened to Roc, but he was there to find out if his son was okay. He walked up to the counter and spoke with the receptionist that asked him to take a seat while she got some information for him. Baraka was both nervous and frustrated because the man Adisa said was taken into custody for the incident was Nika's husband Usian.

Baraka sat down on one of the chairs in the waiting area and pulled out his phone. He called the one person that could help him on the fast track of finding out what had happened, but his call had gone unanswered. It had been a month since Baraka talked with his best friend, Jumba, which seemed quite odd to him. There was a time not long ago where they talked several times a week, only if it was merely to discuss sports. Baraka shot Jumba a text message and hoped that he would respond to it. Also, Baraka made a mental note to make sure he dropped by Jumba's house one day this weekend if his friend wasn't at the hospital.

Baraka was patiently waiting for the receptionist to tell him something, but his nerves were starting to get the best of him. He pulled out his phone and checked it again and again to make sure he hadn't missed any calls. He grunted angrily when he saw an email from one of the vendors they had solicited for Roc and Nika's wedding. Even though the wedding was canceled, people were still requesting partial payment.

"Baraka!" Jumba called out, rushing over to him. "What's going on? I got your urgent message."

"I'm not sure, but Adisa called me, saying that Roc had been assaulted by Nika's husband on some gas station parking lot," Baraka explained. "I don't know why that man is targeting my son, but this shit is going to stop right here, right now!"

"I think I know why Usian might have beat Roc up," Jumba replied uncomfortably. "Nika was in the emergency room the other day, and when Roc saw her... well, let's just say that it wasn't pleasant."

"That still doesn't give him the right to go around assaulting my son!" Baraka protested. "Since I can't sue Nika for backing out of the wedding, I can at least sue her husband for assaulting my son for the second time."

"That could get tied up in litigation for years," Jumba said nonchalantly. "Do you really want to bother?"

Baraka looked at him, surprised. Come to think of it, he was surprised that his old friend hadn't mentioned anything about his potential lawsuit against Subira. Jumba was as outraged as anyone else when Subira announced that Nika had married Usian. However, for some reason, he'd been way too calm.

"How are things going with your lawsuit against Subira?" Baraka asked curiously.

"Well, uhhh... I never filed the suit," Jumba replied uncomfortably. "She went to see Usia at the shop, and after a long conversation, Subira decided to write my wife a check for the amount Abdalla had agreed to pay me."

Jumba gave Baraka a smug look as if he were more superior than he was at this moment. "I would have said something to her on your behalf, but it was Usia who received the check."

"You could have called and asked her if she was willing to give me something out the kindness of her heart."

"You know how difficult Subira can be. Besides, she doesn't like you," Jumba mentioned. "I was lucky that she felt sorry enough for my wife to give us some money. I can't go begging her for other people."

This pissed Baraka off, and Jumba saw it in his facial expression. The conversation was getting rather intense, so Jumba felt it would be best to go find out what was going on with Roc. "Let me go to the back and speak to someone about Roc's condition," Jumba said, fidgeting with his phone. "Give me a few minutes, and I'll be right back."

"You go do that," Baraka said coldly. "I'll be waiting right here."

Jumba disappeared behind the doors to the ER while Baraka looked on. He was pissed off at Jumba's response toward asking Subira to give him a check, and Jumba seemed rather smug when he mentioned she paid him. This situation continued to rub Baraka the wrong way all the way around, and it was about time that he stopped being polite and put some effort in getting some results.

Later That Evening...

Usian clumped through the door with his pride in his hands and love in his heart. The laces to his tennis shoes were in his hand, along with his phone and keys. He was frustrated and tired because unbeknownst to him, Roc had the clerk at the gas station call the police. Now he was looking at an aggravated assault charge, and of course, the bitch ass nigga was going to press charges because he had to go to the emergency room. Also, Roc could sue Usian for damages, and knowing his bitch ass, he was going to go for the money that was promised to him for marrying Nika. However, Usian didn't regret what he'd done, because he was always going to uphold the honor of his wife. Let any nigga step to her incorrectly, and Usian was going to put them in their place with no questions asked.

Usian noticed it was dark in the house, and the only light on was the one in the kitchen. He journeyed down the hallway in search of Nika. He wanted to give her a kiss and tell her about knocking Roc's bitch ass out. She always made him feel better when his day was fucked up. Marrying her was the best thing he'd ever done in his life besides opening up his business. Nika had proven that she was worth the wait, and Usian was going to do whatever it took to keep his wife happy.

He walked into the kitchen and stopped short when he saw Nika standing over at the stove. She was butt ass naked with an apron tied around her waist. Her long, dark-chocolate legs were being held up on a pair of black, patent leather stilettos, and Usian's dick instantly stood at attention. Nika turned around and smiled brightly at him. She licked her lips suggestively then bit the bottom when she saw that Usian was aroused.

"Welcome home, my king," Nika said seductively. "I noticed you're happy to see me." Nika's eyes went down to his erection then came back up to meet his.

"What you got on, baby?" Usian asked, dumping the stuff he was carrying on the table.

"This is a sexy housewife apron," she replied. "This was a wedding gift from my auntie Meme. She said you would appreciate me cooking a meal in it. Do you like it?"

Usian looked her up and down with a seductive smile on his face. The black and white striped apron covered her breasts and stopped midthigh. The black lace trim surrounded the neck and bodice of the garment, and it tied around her waist in a perfect bow. Her hair was curly because she'd taken down her twists, and it was contained with a black, stretchable head-band. "Let me make you a drink, baby. It's all about you tonight, my hero."

"I'm yo' hero, huh?" Usian asked, chuckling.

"Did you really just ask me that question?" Nika replied. "I be trying not to call you a nigga, but damn, baby; you make it so hard for me."

She walked over to the table and picked up a fifth of Usian's favorite cognac while he laughed at her. She broke the seal and popped the top before pouring him a shot in a short glass. "Would you like it on the rocks? I know you like it straight with no chaser."

"Yeah… give me a cube of ice but only one because those big ass squares from that old-school ice tray will water down my drink."

"My mama gave us those ice trays. She's had them for a long time," Nika said, opening the freezer door.

"I bet she brought them back from Africa," Usian mumbled.

"No, smart ass! She got them from the Goodwill."

Nika dropped a cube into his drink and closed the door behind her. "Don't be talking shit, Usian, 'cause yo' ass be loving these ice cubes when your ass come in from being out in the heat."

"You were looking so sexy to me until you started talking shit to me," Usian teased.

"I still look sexy as fuck to you, mister, even if I am talking shit to you," Nika replied, handing him the drink. "Now give me a kiss... nigga!"

Usian took a sip of his drink then licked his lips. He stared at his wife with his eyebrow lifted while she stared him down. "I don't care if you're mad. Give me a kiss, baby."

Usian leaned forward and gave his wife a kiss. Nika slipped her tongue in his mouth, and they tongued each other down nastily. Usian wrapped his arm around her and gripped her butt with his hand. Nika pulled away from him and shimmied all the way down to the floor then came back up with a big smile. She placed her hand upon his cheek and gazed into his soft, brown eyes. "Ew, baby, we have to stop so I can run your bath water. I plan to reward you with a meal fit for a king while you soak in the tub and relax. I appreciate you so much, Usian, and thank you for handling my lightweight."

"I'd knock out the muthafuckin president of the United States if he fixed his lips to disrespect you. You are my world, Nika, and I want you to understand that, baby."

"I do, baby," Nika replied, smiling.

She kissed his lips quickly then pulled away from him. She walked over to the table and picked up a pre-rolled blunt. She fired it up and took a few long pulls off of it.

"Hey! Where's everybody at? Yo' ass walking around here all naked and shit. What if CJ and Precious come in the house?" Usian fussed.

"We don't have to worry about them, baby," Nika said proudly. "I sent they ass with your mother when she came over to check on Precious and CJ."

"She came over here?" Usian asked, surprised.

"She's always over here. You're the one who's never here."

Nika pushed past him, and Usian grabbed her arm. "All of that's going to change soon, Nika, I promise," Usian said, kissing the back of her hand softly. "Give me a couple more months, and we won't have to worry about me being out in the streets anymore."

"You promise?" Nika asked softly.

"I promise," Usian replied, pulling her down to him and kissing her lips firmly.

"Okay, baby," Nika replied, pulling away from him. "Let me go fix your bathwater before we start sexing right here in this chair."

She left out of the kitchen and headed to their room. She had everything planned out for a perfect evening with her husband. While she was drawing his bath, Nika thought about a conversation that she'd had earlier with Precious. For some reason, Precious felt compelled to go to Nika and share whatever information she found out. If Nika told him that Pooh was behind the kidnapping, he was sure to leave the house right now to find him. However, if she fed, bathed, and sexed him really good before she told him, maybe Usian would be too tired to react. Nika giggled and shook her head because she knew her man like the back of her hand. She would rather wait to tell him in the morning after he was well rested. She refused to let her evening be ruined. Besides, he'd handled enough business for one day.

THREE DAYS LATER...

Roc and Pooh were lying in the bed after a few hours of pure fucking. Roc was so frustrated by the embarrassing incident that happed at the gas station with Usian that he hadn't been able to sleep or concentrate, and if that wasn't enough, his father was breathing down his neck about not using the money he had to pay his tuition. He'd gotten as many extensions as he could get, and the balance was due immediately, or else he wouldn't be able to return to the hospital to finish his residency. Shit couldn't get any worse, but Roc wasn't going to hold his breath.

"Thanks for the workout," Roc said, getting up out of the bed.

Sweat was glistening on his muscles from the work he'd put in on Pooh. "I'm going to let you grab a shower in the guest bathroom while I take a shower in here. I wouldn't want Carlos to see us in the shower together, because he might get jealous."

"Nigga, what?" Pooh asked hostilely. "I'm goin' take a shower wherever the fuck I decide."

He got out of the bed and grabbed his clothes off the floor in one big swoop. He pushed past Roc, bumping him in the process, and for some reason, it pissed Roc off. He was tired of people thinking that he was a bitch ass nigga. He was a man, and people were going to respect him, starting right now!

"Nigga, don't bump me!" Roc snapped. "Watch where the fuck you're going!"

"Nigga, fuck you!" Pooh spat, walking into the bathroom. "I don't know who the fuck you think you're talking too!"

"I'm talking to you, bitch ass nigga!" Roc bellowed.

He turned and charged behind Pooh, pushing him into the wall. Pooh turned around and dropped his clothes because Roc had him fucked up. "I'm tired of your dumb ass! You're the reason why I'm in the fucking predicament that I'm in! All you had to do is grab Usian, and none of this shit would be happening!"

Roc aggressively pushed Pooh again, but this time, Pooh swung at Roc, hitting him in the chest. Roc looked down at the spot then back up at Pooh. There was a seriousness in Roc's eyes that made Pooh feel a little uneasy. Roc rushed Pooh, throwing several combinations of punches. He was hitting Pooh in the face and chest in a rotation that had Pooh shook. Pooh kept moving backward in hopes that he would be able to get away from Roc, but the punches were coming too fast. Roc was like a beast dominating Pooh with punches, and the more blood Roc saw running down Pooh's face, the more Roc felt vindicated.

He swung one last time, upper cutting Pooh in the chin. Pooh fell backward and slipped on the bath rug in the process. He tried to catch his balance, but hit his head on the side of the toilet. Blood splattered all over the commode as Pooh's head hit the floor hard. It continued to spill out on the floor as Pooh's body lay lifelessly. Roc stood proudly, feeling triumphant in his victory. He'd gotten his ass beat by Usian twice in two months, and the second time, Roc had to go to the hospital because he had a concussion. "Yo' dumb ass is going to learn how to stay in your fucking place! The next time I tell your ass to do something, bitch ass nigga, you better listen and follow orders!"

Roc walked over and nudged Pooh with his foot, but Pooh didn't move. He leaned over Pooh's body and noticed a pool of blood on the floor up under his head. Roc's eyes widened as he dropped down to his knees. He quickly rolled Pooh over and pressed two fingers up under his chin. There wasn't a pulse, but Roc swore he felt something. He rolled

Pooh flat on his back and began CPR. This couldn't possibly be happening to Roc after everything he'd been through. He couldn't go to jail for murder, and that was what he was going to be charged with when the police found out about their fight. "Wake the fuck up, nigga!" Roc shouted, pressing down on Pooh's chest. "Your bitch ass is always fucking shit up! Wake yo' punk ass up!"

Roc began to sob. "I said wake yo' punk ass up!"

"What the fuck is going on in here?" Carlos asked, walking through the bathroom door. "I heard your ass yelling..."

Carlos stopped in his tracks and froze. Roc was covered in blood, and Pooh was lying on the floor, and he was not moving. "What the fuck, Roc?"

"I... I... I... I think he's dead," Roc stuttered. "He'd pissed me off with his smart-ass mouth, and I wanted to shut him up."

"You should have put your dick in his mouth since you're butt ass naked," Carlos replied, sarcastically. "Come to think of it, Pooh's naked too. What's up with that?"

Roc looked up at Carlos in disbelief. Pooh was lying in front of him dead, and the only thing he could think about was the fact that both of them were naked.

"You're tripping off me being naked, and this nigga is lying here dead!" Roc shouted. "What the fuck is wrong with you?"

"What the fuck is wrong with me? What the fuck is wrong with you?" Carlos yelled back angrily. "You're the one sitting here butt ass naked with blood all over you, screaming Pooh's dead! I take it you're the one who done it, clown ass nigga, so you better watch how the fuck you're talking to me because I'm the one who's going to help your stupid ass!"

"I... I didn't kill him," Roc protested. "He hit his head on the toilet... That's how he died."

Roc rose up off the floor. "Look at the commode. There's blood all over it. The police would be able to see that it was an accident! I tried to do CPR to revive him!" Roc shouted frantically.

"Are you going to explain to them why Pooh is in here naked?" Carlos asked, crossing his arms in front of him.

"I could tell them that he was supposed to be in here taking a shower, but when I came up here to check on him, I didn't hear the shower or get a response when I knocked on the door, so I came in and found him lying on the floor in a pool of blood. I'm a resident at the hospital, so that's why I tried to do CPR to revive him," Roc explained.

"But we're at my house, and they're going to want to know why I wasn't here," Carlos said, walking over to the door.

He glanced into his bedroom and saw that his sheets were messed up. He'd changed them fresh this morning because he and Pooh had messed them up. The bullet wound that Pooh had suffered left stains on the bed each time they had sex, so Carlos knew what was up when he saw the same blood stains on the cover. "It's obvious the two of you were up in here fucking! I asked you not to mess around with Pooh since he's been fucking shit up for us!" Carlos complained. "I was about to come tell you that Pooh was the one who robbed us."

"What the fuck you mean?" Roc asked, puzzled.

"Exactly what the fuck I said!" Carlos retorted. "This nigga named Ed that I do business with asked me why I've been keeping Pooh around me. I told the nigga that he was doing some work for me, and Ed started laughing. He said, 'that nigga was the one who robbed you. You look real good, letting that nigga know all of your business'. I wanted to hit his ass in the face because he was the one who introduced us."

"It's your fault that we're having these problems! I was stupid for letting you talk me into using my loan money to buy fucking drugs! It was you who got us robbed! It was you who brought Pooh into our lives, and now this nigga is lying here dead on the floor!"

"And you're the stupid muthafucka who killed him!" Carlos shouted back. "You need to calm the fuck down so we can figure this shit out! We can't use your story, because thanks to you, Pooh has cuts and bruises on his face."

Roc looked down and frowned when he saw them. "You just couldn't stay away. It was killing you that I was fucking with Pooh!" Carlos hissed. "I was willing to let you marry that bitch, and all I asked was to have a little something on the side."

"I know you're not trying to make this about you," Roc said, fuming. "I needed to let off some steam, and of course, you weren't here. Pooh was lying around in those tight white drawers, and the way they were sucked up in his ass made me hard as fuck. I was coming over for you to satisfy me, so I chose the only option available at the time!"

"Whatever!" Carlos said, rolling his eyes. "You sure as hell didn't call me!"

Pooh's phone started to ring. Both men looked down at it then back up at each other. "Should we turn his phone off?" Carlos questioned.

"Naw... let's leave it on for a little while longer," Roc suggested. "I'm about to go take a shower, and when I get back, we need to figure out what the fuck we're going to do."

"You sure this nigga is over here?" CJ asked, pulling up to the curb.

"This is where the tracker says he's at," Trey replied.

CJ stared at him crazily. "Don't look at me like that nigga! Pooh's bitch ass is scandalous, and I didn't trust the nigga. I put a tracker on his phone to keep up with his ass because he wasn't never going to get the drop on me. I knew where his ass was at, at all times!" Trey bragged. "And now, thanks to me, we know exactly where he's at."

CJ watched the house and noticed one of the cars sitting in front of it. The paint job and rims were what stood out to CJ because it looked real familiar. He took out his phone and snapped a picture of it so that he could remember it the next time he saw it. "What the fuck you taking pictures for?" Trey asked nervously. "Them people can hack our phones and use the picture as evidence."

"Shut yo' bitch ass up, Trey!" CJ said, frowning. "I know what the fuck I'm doing! You better keep a lookout for that nigga Pooh so that we can get his ass! I'm nervous as a muthafucka, but I know what I gotta do. That nigga killed my mama and tried to kill my uncle. He doesn't deserve to live too much longer, and I'm going to be the one to end his life!"

"You sound like Dr. Martin Luther King Jr., nigga! You got a dream! Martin had a dream!" Trey rapped.

CJ swatted Trey on the arm and frowned. "Damn, bruh! Why you hit me? I was just saying—"

"Don't say shit! Just sit the fuck there and fire up that blunt you've been cuffing for the last hour," CJ fussed.

"That sounds like a good idea," Trey said, lighting the blunt.

CJ's phone started ringing, and he snatched it up off his lap. He surveyed the area before looking at the number. "Answer the muthafuckin phone, nigga! That gay ass ringtone is getting on my nervous."

"You're calling my ringtone gay, but you're the bitch ass nigga that's got another man's phone tracked," CJ shot back. "Now you tell me what's the gayest."

CJ's phone stopped ringing as he looked down at it. "Shit! This girl doesn't want nothing."

CJ's text message alert went off. He looked down and swiped on the message from Precious. A smile appeared across his face because he knew she was begging for food.

"You better get used to it. My baby mama is annoying as hell! She's always calling and begging for shit. That's why I've been dodging her ass. She always trying to make a nigga babysit," Trey whined. "I don't have time to be sitting around at her house, watching a kid while she goes to work. I told her ass to put Treylee in daycare, and she had the nerve to get mad at me. Her ass got welfare and Section 8, thanks to me, so she better be grateful that I ain't take our daughter and get that shit myself."

"Shut the fuck up and pass the blunt," CJ said, frowning. "That child is probably better off not being around your dumb ass. Do you realize how stupid you sound? A baby is a blessing, and I'm going to love mine until I breathe my last breath. I don't care if they rob every muthafucka in America. I'm riding for mine, and I hope this nigga Pooh comes out of this house soon so I can go get my bae some food to feed my baby. She wants some Chinese food and a whole list of snacks."

"Her ass has always been greedy, so I know she's eating like a muthafucka now that she's pregnant," Trey mentioned.

"Like a baby bear fresh out its mama's pussy," CJ joked.

They both laughed heartily until someone came out of the house where Pooh was supposed to be at. CJ pushed Trey and pointed as they watched Roc and Craig come out of the house. It was a late Wednesday night, so there wasn't that much traffic on the street. This house was located on the southside of the city, and it wasn't surprising that the street was deserted, because people were held up in their nice, cool homes. It was the dead of summer, and there heat advisory was issued. The two men that came out of the house were arguing, and CJ recognized Roc when he walked to his car—the same car he recognized when they first arrived at the house. CJ wondered if Pooh was still in there. He wanted to sneak up on the nigga when he got him. He swiped the screen of his phone and called Pooh's line. If the nigga was in the house, they were going to go knock on the door once Roc and ole boy pulled off. CJ sat straight up when he saw Roc reach into his pocket and pull out a phone. Roc looked around then answered it, making CJ wonder what the fuck was going on.

"Who is this?" Roc barked.

CJ held the phone as he looked over at Trey and put his finger to his lips. He shook his head from side to side and pointed as both men watched Roc talk on Pooh's phone. CJ hung it up and hit Trey on his arm.

"That nigga answered Pooh's phone. I believe he's in that house, and we're about to go see if that nigga is in there," CJ said, pulling out his gun.

"What if he doesn't answer the door?" Trey asked, pulling out his gun.

"We gon' bust up in the muthafucka!" CJ snapped, turning off the car. "Now get the fuck out!"

CHAPTER

"*B*iiiitch! You've been so neglectful to me friend since you got married," Kimmie complained. "I have to spend my money with you in order to see my supposed best friend."

She rolled her eyes and rocked her head back and forth, making Nika laugh.

"Hold your head still, girl," Nika said, pushing her upside the head. "Now you know you never pay for hairdos, bitch, and I'm sorry that I haven't been available."

"Listen to you... You're not available," Kimmie said, rolling her eyes again.

"Girl, I'm for real! It's a lot of work, being a wife and business owner. I do about three heads a day on average, and I start first thing in the morning. I only do single-braided styles on the weekends because one head of those and a simple braid-up style a day will get me some serious coins."

"Now you know I don't want to hear about your braiding business," Kimmie said, smacking her lips. "I want to hear about the sex you're having with your husband! We didn't even get a chance to talk for real after your wedding night. I know that tight, little twat has loosened up, and you're fucking like a real porn star now!"

—The ladies laughed while Nika gathered some hair to braid into Kimmie's. She loved trying new hairstyles out on her bestie, and Kimmie was the reason she had gotten so many clients. "Do you like sucking dick... and did the techniques I taught you work?"

"You are asking a whole lot of questions, nosy," Nika said, laughing.

She felt a bit uncomfortable talking about her sex life with Usian because she'd never really done it before. Nika was working hard on being a good wife, and Usian told her that their business wasn't to be put out in the streets. He apologized for telling all of his friends that she was a virgin, but now that they were married, all was forgiven. "Kimmie, I..." Nika looked at her bashfully. "Girlllll... that shit feels so muthafuckin good! He makes my toes crack, my back arch, and body shake uncontrollably. You weren't lying though when you told me that the shit was going to hurt the first few times! I almost kneed that nigga in the nuts so I could get the fuck up!"

Both women started laughing heartily. "He told me we had to do it a few more times before it stops hurting, but it still hurts sometimes when he pounds my pussy out, and I love it! I absolutely love it, girl! We have sex several times a day, and I especially love it when he bends me over and hits it from the back!"

"Listen to yo' nasty ass! How do you like sucking dick?" Kimmie asked, reaching into her bag of licorice. "I know I taught your ass well."

Kimmie bit into the piece of candy and chewed it while Nika put a braid in her hair.

"He loves getting head like you said," Nika replied, amazed. "I was a bit clumsy at first, but he grabbed my head and guided my tempo while telling me what to do with my mouth. I was so turned on that I purposely messed up so that he would grip my hair tighter and pump in and out of my mouth."

"Bitch, you can't do that shit like they do on a porno," Kimmie advised. "Trying to be like those bitches will get you fucked around for real!"

Nika laughed and started parting Kimmie's hair. "I'm for real, girl! I tried to do some shit I saw one of those bitches doing and damn near had to go to the hospital. I thought my ass was being split in two when that nigga tried to stick his big dick into my little asshole."

"You don't like anal?" Nika questioned.

"Oh, Lord! He done turned you out that quick!" Kimmie shouted, snatching her head away.

She turned around and looked at her friend in disbelief. "Why you let him gas you up like that?"

Nika laughed, taking a piece of licorice out Kimmie's bag.

"We've never had anal sex, but we've played a few backdoor games," Nika disclosed. "Don't you go running your mouth to Mac about what we've been talking about. The last thing I need is for Usian to be fussing at me about it."

"You know I ain't going to say nothing."

"Girl, please… you can't hold water," Nika said, leaning Kimmie's head over to the side. "Anyway, how are things going with you and Mac? I heard through the grapevine that he's going to ask you to move in with him."

"We've talked about it," Kimmie replied solemnly.

"What's wrong, friend? Why do you sound like that?"

"Because, friend, I miss you," Kimmie admitted. "I need you to be present with me. I was there with you when you were going through all the bullshit with Usian. I was your Pinky, and now I need my Brain."

"Ahhh… I'm sorry, Kimmie," Nika apologized. "I've just been busy, being a wife. I told you all I do is eat, pray, and fuck. I go upstairs and spend time with my mama and aunt, oh and Precious, CJ's baby mama."

"CJ's baby mama!" Kimmie shouted. "When did all of this happened?"

"About four months ago," Kimmie replied, laughing.

The doorbell to her business rang, and Kimmie looked up at the camera. There was a woman in a large hat and big sunglass standing there, and Nika couldn't see her face. "Who the fuck is that?" Kimmie asked, staring up at the screen.

"I don't know, but people ring my bell all the time to ask me questions about pricing," Nika explained. "Can I help you?" she asked, pressing the intercom button.

"Yes, ma'am. I wanted to talk with you about scheduling an appointment and maybe looking at some style books if you have them," the woman replied.

"I'm in the middle of doing braids, and I can't stop to speak with you. I have business cards and flyers downstairs in the furniture store, and it has my Instagram tag on there where you can take a look at my work,"

Nika explained. "Oh... and the phone number is on the door. Thanks for stopping by."

Nika and Kimmie went back to talking, and neither one of them paid any attention to the screen. Nika looked up and noticed the woman was still standing there, and this time, she was peeking through the glass. "This bitch is still standing outside the door."

"What the fuck?" Kimmie said, reaching inside her bag.

"What you grabbing out your bag?"

Kimmie came out of her purse with a small caliber gun. "You're carrying a gun now?" Nika asked, surprised.

"Girl, yeah, and apparently, you need to get you one too!" Kimmie said, getting up from her seat. "When shit got serious between me and Mac, he told me that I had to carry a gun. We went together, and he bought this beauty for me. I'm surprised Usian didn't get you one. He has a gun on him every time I see him."

"He keeps it in his truck when he's at a construction site, but he does keep it in his waistband when he's walking around. However, I don't need a gun," Nika insisted. "Allah is my protector, and if it is his will for me to die, then thy will be done."

"That shit might work for you, but I don't play that shit," Kimmie said, walking toward the door. The woman walked away and headed down the steps while the two women watched her on the screen. She turned and went inside the furniture store, and Kimmie relaxed a little bit. The woman seemed eerily familiar, but Nika decided not to worry about it.

The bell rang as Jessica walked into the furniture store. She was told by a mutual friend that she'd run into Usian at the grocery store with his new wife. The friend went on to mention that the couple just opened a furniture store and that his wife had an African braiding shop above it. Jessica wasn't surprised to hear about the marriage, but she didn't know about the businesses. She questioned the friend if she knew the location of the businesses, and the friend gave her the name of the street where it was located. Jessica got in her car and hurried to the street. She drove down several blocks until she came up on it.

The store front was located on Maffit Avenue off of St. Louis Avenue. She pulled up in front of it, and tears formed in the well of her eyes. The reason she had on the hat and big glasses was her face still had bruising from Nika beating her up that dreadful night. Jessica hid in the house with shame for several days before she finally decided to come outside. Her friends tried to come over and check on her because word got around that she'd gotten beat up. They never mentioned who told them, but she had a suspicion that a certain jilted lover might have run their mouth.

It was difficult for Jessica to acknowledge that Usian was married to Nika. She loved him more than any of the men she'd dated. Usian had a certain way about him that drove Jessica crazy. When she heard that Usian was back in the loop with Whisper, she figured this was the best time to solidify herself with him. He could give her the lifestyle she wanted to live, and her street credibility would go up quite a few notches when people learned that she was Usian's girl.

Jessica got out of the car and decided to go up to the braiding shop first in hopes to seek some revenge on that black bitch. She pulled out some pepper spray and tried to conceal it in her hand. Jessica knew it would be difficult for Nika to recognize who she was in the big hat and sunglasses. It was time for payback, and she wasn't going to be so polite about the situation like Nika. The plan was to go into the shop and get as close to Nika as possible then mace her in the eyes and beat her senseless. There was no way she was going to allow this marriage to thrive without her. If Usian wouldn't accept her as his side piece, then she'd have to get rid of Nika so that she could become his second wife.

"Ma'am, can I help you?" a male voice asked.

Jessica looked up at him and smiled pleasantly. "Welcome to our one of a kind furniture store. What brings you in today?"

"Hi," Jessica uttered, looking around. "Is Usian here?"

"No, ma'am, he's not. Is there something I can help you with?" the man asked, checking her out. The tight-fitting leggings that Jessica had on were gripping all of her curves the right way.

"No," Jessica replied, continuing to look around.

"Well, all of our furniture is one-of-a-kind, made by the owner, Usian. Several of the pieces were inspired by his wife, Nika, and Usian makes customized furniture if there's a one-of-a-kind piece you want made."

Rage filled Jessica's heart as she stared at all of the beautiful couches, chairs, and tables. Why was it that the bitch Nika meant so much to Usian when it seemed like the two of them didn't get along for shit whenever

Jessica was around? A part of her wanted to destroy all of the furniture sitting in the store. How dare Usian treat her like she wasn't shit. She'd done things sexually with him that she wouldn't dare do with another man. Besides, no other man could satisfy her like him. "Excuse me, ma'am… is everything okay?"

"Yes," Jessica replied, wiping tears from her cheek. "I was told by the woman upstairs that I could get a flyer with pricing for her braiding shop."

"You sure can," the man said eagerly. "Let me go grab one for you."

The salesman turned and headed toward the counter. Jessica quickly reached into her purse to find some type of sharp object. "Ma'am! We've seemed to run out of the ones we had on the counter. Let me go to the back and grab a few."

"Okay," Jessica replied sweetly.

She continued to dig around in her junky bag until she came across a metal nail file. She took it out and went over to a red loveseat that was made from some type of velour fabric. She stabbed the seat of the small couch with the file, and it sank down into the cushioning. Next, she dragged it across, making a large tare, but that wasn't good enough for her. She grabbed a piece of the loose fabric and pulled it, ripping the seat of the beautifully crafted furniture.

"Ma'am!"

"Huh?" Jessica called out, startled.

She quickly turned and walked away so that she wouldn't draw any attention to the loveseat. She moved with haste to the man and tried to act cool. "Do you have the flyer for me?"

"Yes, I do," he replied, holding it out.

"Thank you," Jessica replied, snatching it out of her hand. "You have a good day."

"You do the same."

Jessica hurried out the store and didn't look back. She got into her car and started it then smashed off down the street. She told Siri to call Usian, and she waited patiently for the call to be put through. She damn near crashed into the car in front of her at a red light because she'd gotten the message that his phone had been disconnected or no longer in service.

"No!" she cried out. "No… no… no… no! This is not happening to me!"

CHAPTER

*N*ika had been in the kitchen cooking since she'd made it home from the shop. Jabari was coming over for dinner tonight, and she'd invited her mother and Zaida to come down. CJ had gotten a hotel room for himself and Precious for a few days to chill at so everyone would be able to sit and eat comfortably. Nika was looking forward to her first dinner party as Mrs. Jasper Simpson Jr., and the company they were having was a good way to start.

"It smells good in here," Usian said, walking up behind Nika.

"Here... Taste this," she said, holding up a spoonful of whipped sweet potatoes in his mouth.

"Mmmm... mmm... that taste good, baby," he replied, chewing. "You can cook your ass off. I'm glad I married a winner."

"Ah, baby, you're so sweet," Nika said, turning her head and giving him a kiss.

"Mark said some bitch came into the store acting strange today," said Usian, walking over to the refrigerator. "Did anything weird happen at the shop today?"

"Did he say how the woman looked?" Nika asked, moving about the kitchen. "I had some woman come up to the door, trying to get inside. She had on a big hat and large sunglasses, so I couldn't see her face."

"That's the same thing Mark said the woman had on. Also, he said that she asked for me by name," Usian replied. "I wonder who that could be?"

"It might be one of your fans," Nika said, laughing. "You know all those thirsty ass hoes be on you at the lounge, especially since they know you have a wife now."

"That might be true, but I only have eyes for one hoe," Usian replied, grabbing a handful of Nika's butt. He wrapped his arms around her and kissed her lips softly. "I only have eyes for you, baby."

"If you know what's good for you, then you better," Nika replied.

She kissed his lips again softly, and it turned into a full-blown make-out session. Usian slid his tongue inside of Nika's mouth and kissed her nastily for a few minutes. His hands explored her body as he lustfully sucked her bottom lip. Nika was so moist in between her legs that she wanted him to take her right then and there. She slipped her hands down into his jogging pants and stroked his rod slowly. Usian widened his lips and gasped against Nika's because her hands felt like magic from what she was doing. "We have some time before dinner, so we can get a little quickie in," Nika offered.

Before Usian could respond, Nika was already down on her knees with his dick out and her tongue circling the head. She put it in her mouth then pulled it back out, beating it against her lips. Usian looked down at her with lust in his eyes as he bit down on his bottom lip. Nika opened her mouth wide and took all of him inside and deep throated him a few times before sliding the head to the back of her lips. She did this a few more times, tightening her jaws, and Usian was loving every minute of it. He grabbed her hair and started pumping her mouth while Nika continued to bob and slob on his joint. She seemed to become better and better each time she gave him head, and this time was definitely the bomb.

"That's right, baby… Gobble it up," Usian uttered. "Oooouuu, this shit feels so good!"

Nika moaned against the shaft of his dick, and the vibrations made Usian's head fall back. Nika continued to deep throat her husband because she wanted him to cum real hard in her mouth. She knew the moment of truth was coming because she felt his dick tighten in her mouth. She gripped the shaft and stroked him while she continued to go up and down on him. Usian pulled her hair then thrusted hard into her mouth as his load exploded in her mouth. Nika felt his man milk hit against the back of her throat, and she gobbled it up greedily. She licked up and down his rod, making sure she got every inch of his offering as she stared up at him devilishly. "You're a nasty little girl," Usian teased, pulling her up off her knees.

"Papi likes it when I'm nasty, don't you?" Nika teased back, and Usian collapsed his lips on top of hers.

They kissed nastily for a few minutes while Nika jacked his dick. She desperately wanted it inside of her without a moment to waste. "Gosh, bae... you got me so wet and horny."

"You got yourself all worked up," Usian replied, smirking. "But I'm gonna scratch that itch, baby. Turn around for papi one time."

Nika turned around, pulling her leggings down mid-thigh. She bent over, exposing her thick wet folds to him, and he moaned at the sight. Usian couldn't help himself, so he pulled up a chair behind her and sat down. Next, he leaned forward and began feasting on her goodies. He slid his tongue between her lips and pushed in and out, making Nika whimper from the sensations he was providing. He took his finger and rubbed it against her nub, and it damn near sent her over the edge.

Knock, knock, knock!

"Nika!" Subira called out.

"Ma'am!" Nika called back, stiffening her body.

"Is everything alright in there?"

Usian slowly slid his tongue out of her and latched onto her clit. He sucked in real hard, and Nika's knees buckled.

"Daaaaayyyyyuuuummmm..." Nika uttered. "I'm... I'm okay, Mama! Go back upstairs!"

"Okay, baby, but next time, y'all need to go into the bedroom," Subira replied. "And I hope y'all clean the kitchen when you're done. I recommend using a lot of bleach!"

Usian laughed against Nika's money spot, and her eyes rolled into the back of her head. "Oh... and don't forget that you have prayer in less than ten minutes," Subira reminded them.

"Okay, Mama, thank you," Nika replied.

She peeked back at Usian, who was still feasting on her goodies. She wasn't really tripping off prayer time, but if her mother mentioned it, she was probably going to call or come down to remind them again. "Baby, let's go into the bedroom to finish what we've started. The chicken and veggies are roasting in the oven, and the sweet potatoes are ready."

Usian didn't say anything and continued to savor her flavor. Her eyes rolled in the back of her head again when he slid his finger inside of her butthole, and when he pushed it in and out a few times, she orgasmed all in his mouth. "Ahhhh shit, Usian!" Nika called out. "Yessss, bae. Yessssss, bae. Yes, bae!"

Her body shook as she held on to the counter, and Usian wouldn't let up. He continued to suck out all she had to offer, and his greedy ass still wanted more. Nika pushed back on his face then pulled away, standing up to gain her composure.

"What are you doing?" Usian asked, sounding annoyed. "Assume the position!"

Nika looked up at the clock. "Why are you looking up at the clock?"

"Because I have to make a decision," she replied honestly. "I have to decide between giving praises to Allah or having sex with my husband."

Usian looked at her and smirked.

"So who are you going to choose?" Usian asked, lifting an eyebrow.

Nika looked at him sincerely.

"I'm going to choose Allah," Nika replied boldly. "No man will ever come before God, bae. I don't give a fuck who it is."

Usian studied her face for a second before speaking.

"Wise choice," he replied, standing to his feet. "Let's go get cleaned up so that we can pray. Then we'll finish where we left off."

"Sounds like a plan!"

THE DINNER PARTY was in full swing, and everyone was enjoying themselves. Nika had made an excellent dinner, and everyone was enjoying it. She had prepared some roasted chicken breasts on a bed of carrots, yellow squash and zucchini, mashed sweet potatoes with a butter brown sugar sauce, and a mixed greens salad. Her mother and aunt didn't drink alcohol, so she made them a cranberry spritzer that they both loved. She, Usian, and Jabari drank white wine, which Jabari brought over as a gift. Also, he brought Nika's favorite cake, a Miss Hullins split lemon cake. Nika was so happy to have it for dessert that she promised to bake Jabari some special brownies.

Subira sat at the head of the table, watching everyone happily eating and talking. She noticed that Zaida and Jabari were emerged in conversation and had no idea what they were talking about. Nika and Usian were involved in their own conversation as well, but they weren't doing any talking. They were merely making goo-goo eyes and feeding each other food off their plates.

"Did you clean the kitchen like I told you?" Subira asked, staring at the couple.

"Yes, ma'am. I cleaned the kitchen thoroughly," Usian replied, smiling. "I'll try to make sure she doesn't make so much noise next time so you won't have to come downstairs."

Nika elbowed him and held her hand up to her mouth in embarrassment. She couldn't believe that Usian said such a thing to her mother. Nika didn't even like talking about sex with Subira, because it caused all kinds of anxiety when they did.

"It is expected for newlyweds to have a lot of sex," Subira mentioned. "I'm hoping that Amanika misses her period this month so that one of my grandbabies will arrive within the new year."

"What you mean, one of your grandbabies? How many do you expect me to have?" Nika asked curiously.

"I want as many as Allah sees fit to bless you with," Subira replied. "Usian, how many kids do you want?"

Usian was in the middle of taking a sip of his wine. He put his glass down and wiped his mouth with his napkin.

"We've had this discussion, so don't be bashful about it now."

"I'm not bashful about it, Ma. I've spoken to Nika about it, and we've come to an agreement. Nika said that she would give me five kids," Usian replied proudly.

"That's a good number," Zaida added. "Nika's young enough to give you five children. She's in the good range of child-bearing age. I would recommend spacing them out about a year or two because you want to be able to bond with each of your children properly."

"Why don't you have any children, and where is your husband?" Jabari asked, smiling at her.

"My father arranged my marriage," Zaida explained. "However, the man I was promised to was killed, fighting alongside Nika's father."

"Why am I not sorry to hear that?" Jabari asked smugly. "I would love to take you out to dinner. I've enjoyed our conversation."

"I think I might be much too old for you," Zaida replied bashfully.

"How old do you think I am?" Jabari questioned. "I'll give you three guesses, and if you don't answer right, then you'll have to go out with me."

"I am not allowed to date," Zaida said softly. "It is against our religion to date."

"Oh… that's right," Jabari said sadly. "Is there any way you can make an exception?"

"No," Zaida replied firmly. "We are not allowed to have sexual relations with men who are not our husbands. I'm saving myself for my husband, and I pray that he finds me soon."

Jabari looked over at Usian with his mouth wide open.

"You look surprised," Subira said, wiping the sides of her mouth with a napkin. "How old do you think my baby sister is?"

"I don't know… maybe thirtyish?" Jabari suggested. "I'm thirty-four, so you can't be no more than thirty-six… maybe thirty-seven."

"That's a good guess. I'm thirty-six," Zaida gushed. "My little sister Meme is two years younger than me. I thought you were in your late twenties because you look a lot younger than you actually are."

"And you look younger than what you actually are," Jabari replied, smitten. "I love your big, beautiful, brown eyes and your smooth, cocoa-colored skin."

"Wait a minute, Jabari. You're actually hitting on my inna?" Nika asked, lifting an eyebrow.

"What's an inna?" Jabari asked, looking stupid.

"It means aunt in Hausa, our native language," Zaida explained.

"It doesn't matter what it means. You're trying to slide in on my auntie," Nika countered.

"I think you should stay out the way, Nika, and let those two grown people have their conversation," Usian asked nonchalantly. "I've eaten all of my food, and I would like to have some more. Can you please make me another plate, baby?"

Nika was about to say something until Subira butted in.

"I'm with Usian," Subira agreed. "You should be focused on your husband and not worried about Zaida's Kool-Aid."

"What am I hearing right now?" Nika asked, looking back and forth at her husband and mother.

"What she's telling you is to be more attentive to me. Now get up and fix me some more food," Usian replied.

Nika wanted to argue with them, but a part of her knew they were right. It was interesting to see her aunt even engaged in a conversation with a man because normally, she wouldn't speak to anyone, not unless they were family or close friends.

"Do you want a little or a lot, Usian?" Nika asked, getting up from her seat. "Would anyone else like anything while I'm up?"

"No, thank you, dear," Subira replied.

Nika went over to the stove and fixed her husband another plate. She was arguing with Usian and Subira in her head, but again, she knew that the both of them were right. The rest of the dinner was spent discussing Muslim beliefs and customs. Subira explained why she allowed Nika to live without the restrictions, and Nika shared her conflicts about the two. Zaida shared her envy of Nika and how she got a chance to make her own decisions for her life. The conversation lasted well into the evening until it was time for them to go pray. Jabari left happy with a piece of cake, a smile on his face, and Zaida's phone number.

TWO WEEKS LATER...

"I see they took the boards down off the windows on the house next door," Nika said, passing Usian the blunt. "I've seen men coming in and out of there for the past four months, and I wondered what they were doing inside of there."

"Your nosy ass didn't go over and question them?" Usian asked jokingly.

"You know I wanted too, but I didn't want to hear your big ass mouth."

Usian looked over at his wife and laughed.

"You don't seem to have problems when I put this big ass mouth on your pussy," Usian shot back.

"I sure don't," Nika countered. "And to be honest with you, bae, I love that shit!" They both laughed as Usian passed Nika the blunt back. "As a matter of fact, I want you to put that muthafucka in its place right now!"

"Come here then," Usian suggested, biting his bottom lip.

Nika got up from her seat and walked over to her husband. She leaned down and kissed his lips when a car pulled up in front of their house and blew. They both looked out into the street to see who it was blowing at them. Usian stood up from his chair when he saw CJ letting down the window of a brand-new black Dodge Charger. "Where you get that from?" Usian asked, looking surprised.

"I just cashed out at the car lot and bought it, Unc," CJ announced.

He pulled over to the curb, and Precious was sitting right next to him, smiling like she was in a parade. Usian and Nika walked down the steps and headed toward the sidewalk. Usian naturally grabbed Nika's hand as they strolled to go see CJ's new car.

"Look at y'all ass walking hand and hand," CJ teased. "I want to be like y'all when I grow up."

"Me too!" Precious said, getting out of the car. "Do you like our car?"

"It's nice," Usian replied, giving it a once over. "I don't know why you were stupid enough to go pay cash for a car. That's a good way to get them people to take notice of you. You weren't thinking smart, were you?"

"Unc, relax," CJ said, putting his arm around his uncle's shoulder. "I paid for this car with the money I got back from my mama's life insurance policy. She had a term life for 250 thousand dollars that was split up between me and my brother. I bought a car, and I'm going to use the rest to pay for Precious to go to nursing school. I got a full-ride scholarship, and as long as I keep my grades up, college will pay for itself. Precious, on the other hand, has to wait and apply for her scholarships all over again once she has the baby, so I'm willing to put the money in the bank and take care of my baby mama's tuition."

"Please don't refer to her as that," Usian said firmly. "I hate to hear people refer to their child's mother as a baby mama. We will respect our women around here."

A smile came across Precious's face as she looked over at CJ. "And did you talk to Precious about what we discussed?"

"Yes, and she's down with it," CJ replied. "Actually, she was happy when I told her."

"Told her what?" Nika questioned.

Usian looked over at her and smiled.

"Give me a minute, and I'll show you," Usian replied. "CJ, come go in the house with me so I can ask you something."

"Okay, Unc," CJ replied.

The men disappeared down the sidewalk as Nika and Precious admired the car.

"Get in, Nika, so I can take you for a ride around the block," Precious suggested.

"Okay," Nika said, walking around to the passenger side. "I hope your ass can drive."

"I'm a good driver," Precious said, putting on her seat belt.

She adjusted the seat so that her feet could touch the peddles. "You know I'm short, so I have to scoot up to the steering wheel."

"I have to adjust the seat when I drive Usian's truck," Nika replied. "I see things are going well with you and CJ."

"Yeah... a little," Precious replied. "He's been acting weird for the past two weeks. Ever since him and my brother went out to get us something to eat, the both of them have been acting paranoid."

"Really? For what?"

"I don't know," Precious replied. "They always seem nervous and jumpy. CJ checks his mirrors a thousand times when we're riding down the street."

"Usian hasn't mentioned anything to me," Nika said, watching Precious closely. "Do you think they might have robbed someone? Is that why CJ went out and got a new car?"

"They didn't rob anyone, and the money for the car did come from his mother's life insurance policy," Precious assured her. "But something happened, and the old car has something to do with it."

"You be careful, you hear me?"

"Oh, I am," Precious replied, holding up a gun. "CJ keeps a strap in the car, and I know how to use it too!"

The women hit a couple of blocks and stopped at the gas station around the corner from the house. Precious was hungry and wanted some snacks, and Nika had the munchies, so it was right on time for her. She called Usian to see if he wanted anything, and naturally, he had a list of items. Nika laughed, teased, and cracked a few jokes on him, but she grabbed everything he wanted and few extras of his favorites. She loved being his wife because of the way he loved her mind, body, and spirit, and it was her pleasure to do the little things that made her man happy.

Precious pulled up in front of the house and parked the car. CJ and Usian were sitting on the porch, talking, while they waited for the women to come back from the gas station. He got up and walked down the pathway toward the gate as Nika was coming through with a grocery bag full of stuff. She smiled warmly at CJ and went straight to Usian. She handed him the bag and sat down on his lap.

"I got everything you asked for and something extra," Nika explained.

"You got me something extra? Thank you, baby," Usian said, reaching his face up for a kiss.

Nika leaned down, and their lips pressed together softly. She slid her tongue in quickly and pulled it back out before she sat up. "Damn, baby, you gon' do me like that?"

"You know if I kiss you like that, your dick is going to get hard, and I'm sitting on your lap."

"These are the moments where I miss those short skirts. Do you think that you could indulge me sometimes and wear one on occasion?" Usian asked, smiling.

"I can wear a skirt that stops at my knee. I'm trying to be modest and only expose my body to you, my husband. Isn't this what you wanted, bae? We agreed that I would change up the way I dress, but it has to be respectful in regard to you."

"I know, baby, but I miss them little shorts and those short skirts with those six-inch heels."

"I wear high heels for you all the time," Nika insisted. "Just last night, I wore those blue, patent leather stilettos that you like. You said they lift my ass and make my pussy sit up just right so you don't have to bend your knees."

"I love those damn shoes," Usian said, smiling. "I think we're going shopping tomorrow so you can get about four more pairs of those muthafuckas."

"There's not enough space to put all of the shit that you've already bought me, so where are we going to put them? You have just as many clothes and shoes, if not more than me, so how is this going to work?" Nika asked, laughing. "Oh... and what were you, CJ, and Precious talking about earlier? Don't think I forgot."

"I haven't forgotten anything," Usian replied dryly. "Why don't you get up so I can show you?"

"Okay," Nika replied, getting up off his lap. "And bae, I don't want you to think that you have to spend a lot of the money you received on me. I have my own money, and I'm trying to figure out how I can spoil you. You're so simple to make happy that I don't believe any expensive gift would be sufficient, especially since you already have all the expensive watches that you wanted."

Usian laughed, grabbed the bag of snacks, and stood up on the bottom step. He took Nika by the hand, and they walked down the path toward the gate. He thought it was sweet of his beautiful wife to say that to him, but he wasn't trying to hear shit she was saying. He hadn't even touched any of that money and planned on investing the majority of it in the stock market. Subira was helping him get his illegitimate money into the bank, so he was definitely a millionaire for sure. The one thing he wanted to do for Nika was spoil her because she gave Usian his ability to love someone with his heart instead of using her as a sexual object.

"Baby, you can't tell me how to spend my money," Usian replied, looking sternly at her.

"Don't look at me like that, Usian, because it makes me wet when you do that," Nika disclosed.

"Any look I give your ass makes you horny."

"This might be true, but that one definitely does it for me," Nika replied, biting her bottom lip.

"I think I liked you better when I was only eating your pussy," Usian said, stopping.

He turned to face his wife and smiled warmly as he gazed into her eyes. "Baby, I'm going to buy you whatever I want. I'm going to spoil you with gifts and my love for the rest of your life, so you better get used to it. Now give me a kiss."

Nika didn't respond and did as she was told. She pressed her lips against his as her heart fluttered and skipped a beat. Usian pulled away from her and kissed her lips quickly once more. He had a surprise for his wife, and it was going to be awesome.

The couple strolled out of the gate, and CJ was wiping off the car. Usian laughed as they walked past because he remembered when he had gotten his real car.

"Don't wipe the color off the car, neph. You just got the muthafucka!" Usian joked.

Everyone laughed as Usian and Nika came out the gate and walked down the sidewalk. Nika swung their hands back and forth, and on occasion, Usian would lift it and kiss the back of her hand. Those were the little things that Nika loved, and she hoped that this would last forever. They arrived in front of the house next door, and Usian turned onto the pathway leading up to it with Nika in tow.

"What are we doing over here? We're about to ask the people if we can take a look inside of it?" Nika asked. "My nosy ass sure does want to go up in there and take a look."

Usian didn't say anything as they walked up the steps. Nika was looking all around the front of the house as if she'd never seen it before. "This is a big, beautiful house. I asked my mother why she didn't buy this house instead of the two-family flat, and she said that your mother sold her the building. I remember we were living in a two-bedroom apartment on Saint Louis Avenue before we moved over here. I lowkey love our house, but I don't want to live up under my mama forever," Nika admitted.

"And we're not," Usian replied.

He inserted the key into the deadbolt to unlock the door, then he put it in the handle to open it. He pushed the door open and stepped to the side so that Nika could go in first. She stood staring at him crazily because she wondered, how the hell did he do that?

"What are you doing with a key to this house, bae?" Nika asked curiously.

"I bought it several months ago, and it's my wedding gift to you," Usian uttered nonchalantly. "I planned on getting all the renovations done before we moved up in here, but with CJ and Precious living with us and having a kid, I thought it would be best to let them have the apartment, and we'll move in the house while me and my crew finish working on it. I've already talked to Ma about it, and she thinks it's an excellent idea."

"Did she know you bought this house?"

"Yes," Usian replied, smiling. "I bought it from her. She purchased it when the Sullivan's told her that they were selling it. Ma figured you would be marrying that asshole sooner or later, so she was going to give it to you as a wedding gift."

"So why did you buy it from her?"

"Because I wanted to do something meaningful for us. Your mother has given us so much already, and I wanted to buy our first house. We're going to make so many memories in here, and we have enough bedrooms for five kids to have their own room. I'm going to turn the garage into a workshop for my furniture. I have a room set off in the back of the house where we're going to build you a library. I know you love reading books, and I want you to have every book you could ever want."

Nika pressed her lips against Usian's to make him stop talking. She was so overwhelmed with happiness that she thought her heart would burst.

"Go in yo' house with all of that!" Subira yelled from their porch. "We don't want to see that!"

The couple pulled away and started laughing. They both looked over at Subira, and Usian waved at her. CJ and Precious were laughing too as they looked on.

"Shall we go in and take a look around?" Usian asked.

"Are you going to carry me over the threshold?"

Usian swooped Nika up and threw her over his shoulder. He swatted her on the ass, and Nika laughed uncontrollably. "I wasn't talking about like this, bae!"

"I'm going to carry your ass in here like a savage because you're about to get fucked like one," Usian replied devilishly.

"Well, what are you waiting on?"

Two Months Later...

"I'll get it," Baraka said, walking up to the door.

He looked through the peephole and noticed two well-dressed men standing behind it. He unlocked the door and pulled it open, staring at them strangely. "Can I help you?" Baraka asked frankly.

"Yes. Does a Paki Abioye live here?" one of the men asked.

"He does, but what is this about?" Baraka demanded.

"Sir, who are you to Paki?"

"I'm his father," Baraka replied. "Is there something I can do for you?"

"I'm Detective Smith, and this is my partner, Detective Jackson. We would like to speak with Paki about a suspicious incidental death that happened at a friend's house."

Baraka looked at him strangely.

"Roc never mentioned any of this to me. When did this happen?" Baraka asked. "And I would like to see some credentials."

"No problem," Detective Smith replied. "We're familiar with your legal work, Abioye. The law firm you work at is well known through the department."

"You must be speaking of our criminal law attorneys. I work in corporate law," Baraka mentioned.

The two detectives presented Baraka with their credentials, and he welcomed them into the house. He showed them into the living room and offered them a seat. "Roc is in the theater room with his friend Carlos. Let me go get him."

"Mr. Hadley is here as well?" Detective Jackson asked.

"Yes. He and my son are best friends," Baraka replied. "They've been friends since college."

The detectives looked at one another then back at Baraka. "What was that look for?"

"Nothing really," Detective Smith replied. "The incident happened at Mr. Hadley's apartment. A call was made, and a young man was found dead in his bathroom. Apparently, the victim hit his head on the toilet and died from his injury."

"Okay, but why do you need to speak with my son? I'm sure he didn't have anything to do with it. You should be questioning Carlos," Barak said defensively.

"We would like to speak to him as well, but your son will do for now, Mr. Abioye. Can you go get Paki for us?"

"Why don't we all go down to the theater room together. That way, you can speak with both men," Baraka suggested.

The two detectives looked at him then looked at one another. "There's another room that you can use if you don't want to speak with the men separately."

"That sounds good. Lead the way," Detective Jackson replied.

The two detectives followed Baraka down into the lower level of the house. It was completely finished, and you couldn't tell that it was a basement. Baraka walked over to the door and opened it up. It was relatively dark inside, and the only light was the one from the projector. The room was surrounded with various couches and chairs. The back of someone's head could be seen on the leather couch. Baraka thought it was strange, so he turned on the light and Carlos's head popped up. The two detectives looked at one another as Baraka stared at Carlos and Roc furiously. Both of their clothes were disheveled, and they quickly tried to fix them.

"What's up, Pops?" Roc asked nervously.

He wasn't sure how much his father witnessed, but Carlos was giving him some of the best head of his life, and he hoped that they weren't caught.

"There are two detectives here that would like to talk to you about a person dying in Carlos's house!" Baraka barked back. "Why didn't you mention this to me, son?"

"Because I didn't think it was anything important. A friend of ours was high and drunk when he went to take a shower, and he must have fell and hit his head on the toilet," Roc explained.

He waited a minute then stood up, facing the detectives. "What can I do for you, detectives?"

"We would like to speak to you in private, Paki," Detective Smith replied. "The information we're about to discuss is sensitive to the case, and it would be best to do it privately."

"I have nothing to hide, so we can speak out here in front of everyone," Roc replied confidently.

He was nervous as hell and didn't want to talk to them. He damn near cracked under pressure when he had to give a statement the night in question. He shoved his hands down in his pockets and pinched his leg in anticipation to what was about to happen.

"Fine. We'll do it your way," Detective Jackson replied. "Paki, can you tell us how your semen got into the anal cavity of the deceased?"

"Wait a minute! What!" Roc blurted out. "I don't know what you're talking about, Detective."

"So you're denying having sexual intercourse with Mr. Thomas? We found you, Mr. Thomas, and Mr. Hadley's DNA on the sheets and comforter that were on the bed. Also, Mr. Hadley's DNA was found in the anal cavity of the deceased."

"Me and Pooh were messing around, so my nut should have been down his throat as well," Carlos replied smugly. "I had sex with Pooh the morning in question. He spent the night over my house."

"Carlos... you're gay?" Baraka asked, confused. "Why wasn't I aware of this?"

"The same reason you didn't know that your son was gay!" Carlos announced boldly. "We've been lovers since college, but Roc was too afraid to tell you."

"Roc, is this true!" Baraka thundered. "There is no way my son is a homosexual! He was engaged to be married to a beautiful girl, and I've seen him go out with plenty of women."

"That was only for show, hunty. Your son is gayer than the rainbow flag flying in front of gay bars," Carlos mocked. "Roc, it's time that your father knows the truth. You didn't want to marry Nika, and I think Baraka needs to know how you feel."

Roc didn't speak a word. He was too mortified that his father found out this way. Roc figured after he'd gotten his license, he and Carlos could go as far away from his parents as possible. Roc ultimately planned on his parents not finding out because he didn't want to be disowned.

"It was not your place to out me!" Roc said angrily. "I should have been the one to tell my own father!"

"I'm sorry, Roc, but I'm tired of living in the shadows with you. I can no longer keep this secret and live this lie. You know I'm in love with you, and you're in love with me!" Carlos retorted.

"Excuse me, fellas. I'm sorry to break up your little outing party, but we need to ask some more questions about this case because it seems like Mr. Thomas was murdered. He had fresh bruising and lacerations on his face that were bloody, and do you know anything about Mr. Thomas being shot? He had a bullet wound that had been attended too, but when we checked with all the local hospitals, no one seemed to have any record of him coming into the ER."

"I was the one who fixed up the wound," Roc confessed. "He'd gone over Carlos's house and asked him to call me. I came over and checked the wound out. I removed the bullet and gave him some antibiotics so an infection wouldn't set up."

"Do you know who shot him and why he was shot?" Detective Smith asked.

"He said something about getting into an argument with some friends of his. What's their names?" Roc asked, looking over at a disgruntled Carlos. "What are the two guys' names, Carlos?"

"Trey and CJ," Carlos replied.

He saw how Roc was trying to flip it because when they got back to the house, the front door had been forced open. That was why Carlos called the police and said that his house had been broken into, and they found Pooh lying in the bathroom dead. "Remember the reason why I called was because the house had been broken into, and we found Pooh dead in the bathroom."

"Do you think the two of them might have had something to do with it?" Detective Jackson asked curiously. "Because we did lift one of their fingerprints off your front door, but we didn't find them anywhere else in the house."

"They had to be the ones who did it," Carlos replied. "We still haven't found Pooh's phone anywhere in the house. I remember hearing Pooh say something about them robbing niggas for their phones."

Both detectives had been writing down the information that Carlos and Roc had given them. Detective Jackson remembered seeing Roc's knuckles busted up, but Roc told him it was because he'd gotten into a fight with his ex-fiancé's husband.

"Has your hands healed up, Paki?" Detective Jackson asked.

Roc looked down at his knuckles before looking up at the detective.

"They sure looked like you worked someone out fiercely. Could it be you got into an argument with him about Carlos? Maybe you wanted Carlos for yourself because you got tired of sharing him."

"That's enough!" Baraka interrupted. "If you have any more questions, then you'll have to do it with Roc's attorney present!"

"That won't be necessary, Mr. Abioye. I believe we have all that we need right now," Detective Jackson replied. "Smitty, you got anything?"

"Naw, boss," Detective Smith replied. "I would advise you to stay local. We're definitely going to have more questions for you after we go pick up the young man whose prints were on the door. You better hope this situation doesn't get flipped back on you."

"We're innocent, officer," Roc replied frankly. "And we've been nothing but cooperative with you."

"You have," Detective Jackson replied. "But you know that doesn't mean shit. Criminals are always helpful when they're trying to keep the trail off of them."

"That's enough!" Baraka yelled. "You two need to leave my house immediately!"

"We're leaving," Detective Smith said amusingly. "And we're sorry that you had to find out that your son is gay like this. I know it has to be difficult."

If looks could've killed, then Roc would be dead because his father threw him a look so vicious that he should have fell to his death on the floor from it. "I'm going to need both of you two to come down to the station so we can get samples of your DNA from the both of you for full verification."

"They'll be down there shortly," Baraka replied, walking toward the door.

"Roc, you need to get all of your shit and be out of my house in the next hour," Baraka mentioned before walking out of the room.

The detectives looked at Roc and Carlos before leaving out behind Baraka. Roc put both hands against his face and swiped them downward in disbelief. His whole life was spiraling out of control right in front of him, and there was nothing he could do about it.

"Are you okay?" Carlos asked, touching Roc's cheek, but Roc swatted his hand away and stared at him in disgust. "Don't look at me like that!"

"This is all of your fault!" Roc shouted. "I have to leave my home because your big-mouthed ass had to say something! It was not your place to say shit, but I guess you're satisfied with yourself because you outed me in front of my father! I told you he was going to disown me if he found out, but you don't seem to give a fuck!"

"Because I don't!" Carlos shot back. "I was getting tired of hiding in the wings until you felt like you were ready to tell him! I know you love me, Roc, just as much as I love you! You don't have to live in this sterile house; you can come live with me."

"Do you honestly think I could live at your house after I killed Pooh there?" Roc asked angrily. "I haven't been able to rest since it happened. Why do you think I asked you to come out here to give me some head? I can't stand being at your house, but I guess I'm being forced there."

"So you're being forced to come to my house now?" Carlos asked in disbelief. "You're something else, Paki Abioye, but you've got me fucked up! I see why Nika didn't want to marry your tired ass; you're too afraid to be a man!"

"Fuck you!" Roc said, shoving Carlos in the chest.

"No... fuck you!" Carlos replied, shoving Roc back.

The men started tussling, and they tripped over the ottoman. They fell to the floor, but neither one of them stopped. Roc managed to climb on top of Carlos, pinning him down on the floor. Both of them were breathing heavily as they stared angrily at one another. "Let me up, ole bitch ass nigga!"

"No, fuck you!" Roc replied.

Carlos hawked and spat a wad of mucus in Roc's face. Roc's eyes widened in rage as the glob of mucus dangled off his cheek, and he glared at his lover. He wanted to be mad at Carlos for all the strife that he'd caused in life, but for some reason, he was turned on by all of the aggression.

"Let me up, bastard!" Carlos yelled.

"Shut the fuck up!" Roc yelled back before leaning down and pressing his lips against Carlos's. This was the first time that Roc realized how freeing this actually was. If his father couldn't accept the fact that he was gay, then fuck him! Roc was done hiding who he was from his father, but he still was nervous about Pooh's death because the detectives were too close for comfort. Baraka went back downstairs to speak with both Roc and Carlos privately without the detectives. Their stories sounded sketchy, and Baraka wanted to address the pressing issue that the men were lovers. Their religion forbade the gay lifestyle, and if Roc was over in Africa, Baraka probably would've killed him. He was going to disown his son, but he at least wanted to get him out of this trouble before he completely cut him off.

Baraka went to the door and saw Roc sitting on top of Carlos, and they were engaged in a very intimate kiss. Baraka didn't know what to do or say, so he backed away from the door and disappeared back up the steps.

CHAPTER

Fourteen

$\mathcal{U}$sian was sitting at the bar, having a drink. He had been doing some work on their house, and everyone who was helping had been going hard. He appreciated all of their hard work and decided to buy them a couple of rounds at the lounge. He had been sitting in the same spot since he'd arrived because Nika texted him and asked if he could come pick her up at the shop once she was done with her client's hair. Precious had been going down to the shop in order to learn how to braid hair. Nika was happy that Precious expressed interest in learning how to braid, and she was more than happy to do it. It reminded her of when her auntie Meme handed down the technique and taught her when she was ten. Nika was a little bitty thing, standing on a crate to help her aunts braid hair. This was a skill that was passed down from generation to generation because this was what their family was known for in Africa besides being midwives.

Usian looked at his phone and saw it was past eight o'clock at night. It was taking Nika longer than he anticipated, and his stomach was starting to growl. He knew that Nika wasn't going to make dinner, because it was too late at night, so he decided to order some food from the Chinese restaurant up the street to take home for them to eat. He would surprise Nika and avoid the argument of what they were going to eat for dinner. He learned that Nika liked for him to take charge with other things besides the bedroom. She was always making the domestic decisions, and it was refreshing when he did it for her every once in a while. Usian was going to call the order in but decided to walk up the street instead and place the order that way.

"Lay, I'm headed up the street to get some food. You cool?" Usian asked.

"I've told you to stop offering my wife food," Byrd replied, joking.

"Dude, I used to babysit your wife when she was a little girl, and if I wanted her, nigga, I could have had her, remember that, bruh."

Byrd and Lay laughed at Usian as he walked toward the front door. "Tell your daddy that I went to get some food. Nika should be calling shortly, so I can't hang out with his ass all night."

"Nika got that ass on a curfew, huh?" Lay joked.

"The only thing on a curfew is this... Lay, stop talking to me," Usian urged. "You almost had me say something inappropriate to you."

Lay and Byrd laughed again, and this time, Usian joined in. "Not another word! I'll be back!"

"Okay," Lay replied, taking his empty beer bottle and glass from in front of his spot.

Usian went out the door and headed down the street. It was a hot summer night, and he was ready to go home and take a cool shower with his wife and make love to her under the falling water. He wanted to get a shower wall put into their master bathroom at the new house like the one that was at the Four Seasons Hotel. They'd have to tear the wall out and do some other reconstructive things to the bathroom, but it would be well worth it. They could sleep in one of the other bedrooms while the remodeling took place. The house had three and a half bathrooms, and Usian planned on adding one more downstairs when he finished the basement. That was going to be his man cave and the place where he and Nika would go to hide from the kids when they had them. Usian was deep in thought as he headed down the street to the restaurant. He reached into his shirt pocket and noticed he had a blunt in it. He pulled it out and stopped to fire it up when someone called out his name. He didn't look up until it was completely lit, and when he did, he rolled his eyes up in his head.

"What's up, Smitty, maaaaannnn... I ain't seen you in a month of Sundays," Usian said, hitting his blunt.

"I see you're still moving around through the neighborhood," Smitty replied.

"Yeah, a little bit," Usian replied. "I've been doing some work on some of Big Lee's properties, so I've been in the neighborhood during the day more than usual. I live not too far from here, but I think you already know that."

A car pulled up behind the detective's car and blew. The person in the car was very irate, cursing and shouting obscenities at him. Smitty put on his police lights and waved the person around him. He wasn't about to pull his car over, so they needed to get in the other lane. "Yo' ass blocking traffic to talk to me. Somebody might think that I'm snitching."

"People know your ass ain't saying shit! You did ten years flat, so if you were going to talk, then that would have been the time," Smitty replied, laughing. "But I do need to talk to you about something. Somebody told me Calvin Simpson Jr., AKA CJ, was your nephew. Is that true?"

"Yeah, that's true," Usian replied. "That's my big brother Calvin's son."

"Get the fuck out of here! His son is following in his father's footsteps."

"What do you mean by that?" Usian asked, lifting an eyebrow. "My nephew's been keeping his nose clean since his mama got killed."

"It's funny you should mention that because word on the street is that some nigga named Pooh that we found dead in someone's house was the one who killed your nephew's mother," Smitty offered.

"I don't know who killed his mother, and I really don't care, to be honest. I've hung up all that shit, Smitty, and got married to a beautiful, smart woman."

"She can't be too smart if she married you," Smitty shot back sarcastically. "And quit shitting me, Usian. I know you're back handling things for Whisper. People run their mouths too much around here for my liking, and you know as long as I got something to give, people are going to chat me up."

"You still shaking cats down, Smitty? You're a detective now. You don't have to result in petty beat cop antics. I'm an honest, hardworking man, so you need to come at me with another angle."

"How about we found your nephew's fingerprints on the door handle of the house where Pooh's body was found. There were signs of forced entry, and his prints were on the door handle, and before you respond, two men said that CJ and his friend Trey had beef with Pooh. He did kill CJ's mama."

"So what you gon' do? Lock him up?" Usian asked, hitting his blunt. "He's got a baby on the way, and that nigga can't afford to be locked up for some bullshit that I know he didn't do. What is it that you want?"

"I want him to come down to the station to answer some questions. We don't think that your nephew killed Pooh, but he might have some information to help us. Do you know some dude named Paki, but they call him Roc? He has a best friend named Carlos; well, they're actually lovers, come to find out, but at any rate, know them?"

"Naw, Smitty, I don't know them," Usian said, looking around. "They're not from around here."

"Nope, they're not. I wanted to know if your nephew saw something or if he was up in there with Pooh. People said CJ used to run around with Pooh, so he might know if Pooh was messing with one of the men."

"What you mean, messing with one of the men?" Usian asked, frowning.

"Pooh was getting fucked by both men, and they were all involved in a love triangle," Smitty replied. "I'm not supposed to be telling you this shit, but I want you to understand that I'm not after your nephew. I just want to talk to him to get some verification on some shit."

Usian's phone started ringing, and a smirk came across his face. He was hoping that it was Nika saying that she was ready because he was ready to go home. He reached into his pocket and pulled it out and held the phone up in front of his face. He saw that the security company that he'd hired for the shop was calling. "What's wrong?" Smitty asked, taking a cue by the look on his face.

"I don't know," Usian replied, answering the phone. "Hello."

"Mr. Simpson, this is Donna from Applegate Securities. There's a fire at the furniture store, and the fire department has been dispatched to the scene. Also, an ambulance was called to the scene as well, and it would be best if you got there pronto."

"Fuck!" Usian shouted. "Okay, I'm on my way."

Smitty heard a call over the airways while Usian was on the phone. He figured the call must have had something to do with it because Usian seemed up in arms. "Look, Smitty, my fucking store is on fire!"

"That's you down off of Saint Louis Avenue?"

"Yeah! And my wife was at the muthafucka!" Usian didn't say another word. He turned and ran down toward the lounge. Whisper was coming out the door to find him when Usian ran past him.

"Aye, bruh!" Whisper called out.

"My fucking store is on fire, and Nika's there!" Usian yelled.

Whisper ran behind his homeboy because he was going too. Usian made it to his truck and popped open the locks. Whisper was grabbing the handle when he heard the truck start up. Usian looked over at Whisper and unlocked his door. He appreciated his friend going with him because he had a bad feeling in the pit of his stomach. "Fire this half of a blunt up because I have a feeling that I'm going to need it," Usian said, handing it off to Whisper.

"Put that shit back in your pocket. I was coming to find you to fire this bitch up with you," Whisper explained, holding up a blunt. "CJ called and told me to find you because your phone was going straight to voicemail."

"I was on the phone with the security company," Usian explained. "Also, I was hollin' at Smitty. He ran the whole situation down about me being back out here. Some muthafucka is running their mouth, and that's the sign that I needed to sit the fuck down like I was doing before. I have a wife now, and I'm trying to pump her ass full of kids and grow old with her crazy ass. CJ's straight and about to go to college. Maybe I can let his ass work at the furniture store, or maybe you can find something for him to do with your brothers-in-law."

"Or you can let him keep doing his job. Let him be the one to decide what he's going to do," Whisper suggested, passing the blunt.

"His ass is hotter than a firecracker!" Usian replied, taking the blunt. "I was talking to Smitty, and they want to talk to CJ about a murder."

"A murder?"

"A murder!" Usian replied before hitting the blunt.

Usian ran down the conversation that he'd had with Smitty. He told him about Roc being gay and that Carlos was his lover. He explained that Pooh was messing around with both of them and somehow ended up dead in the house. Smitty was on Big Lee's payroll, so Usian had nothing to worry about. However, Usian never trusted any police, because it was a dirty cop that set him up.

It took the men five minutes to get around to the store. The street was blocked off, so they had to park and walk down a couple of blocks. He saw two ambulances sitting with the fire engines, and his heart sank down into the pit of his stomach.

"Nika!" Usian yelled as he took off running down the street.

Whisper followed closely behind as the two men dodged random people standing around, watching the scene on the street. Usian tried to run up toward the store, but a police officer stopped him in his tracks. Usian tried to ignore the cop, but he grabbed Usian by the arm, stopping him from moving.

"You cannot go up there!" the police ordered. "It's dangerous, and the building is burning badly."

"I'm the owner of the building, and my wife was up in there! Was anyone hurt?" Usian asked, pacing.

"There were two women pulled out of the building. I believe they both are okay, but they suffered smoke inhalation. Go check with EMS. They can tell you better than I can."

"Step back!" one of the firemen shouted, running back himself.

You could see and hear pieces of the roof collapsing down into the building. A cold chill went through Usian's body, and he shook as he watched his dream go up in flames. Whisper put his hand on Usian's shoulder and gripped it.

"Let's go check on Nika," Whisper suggested. "This building is materialistic shit, and y'all can get that back easily. I know you poured your heart and soul into making that furniture, but, bruh, Allah is great, and a thousand more blessings are going to come from it."

"You're right," Usian replied solemnly. "I need to find my wife."

The ambulance closest to them pulled off with the lights flashing and sirens going. The other followed suit, but it was going a different way. "Hold the fuck up!" Usian shouted, running after it. "My wife is in there!"

"Usian! Uncle Usian!" CJ called frantically. "Uncle Usian! Whisper!"

CJ was running full speed toward them, and it looked like he had been crying. His hands were shaking, and his clothes and face were full of soot. He smelled of smoke, and it was very overwhelming.

"What happened to you?" Usian asked, studying his nephew.

"Unc, we need to get to the hospital. I had to drag Nika and Precious out of the burning building," CJ explained. "Someone had barricaded all of the door so that they couldn't get out. The doorknob on the front door was broken off so it was impossible for them to escape. I had to break the front window to get to them. The old man that lives across the street came to help me. He said some woman came in a black car, got out, and went around back. He said he didn't pay it any mind, because people go through the back to get to the braid shop. He told me that he'd gone into the house to grab a beer, and when he came out, the woman had broken out all the windows of the furniture shop and had ran up in there."

"A woman?" Usian questioned.

"A woman," CJ replied. "He said he went across the street to see what was going on, but by the time he made it over, there the crazy woman was running up out of there. He said the next thing he knew, flames had engulfed the walls, and the furniture store was on fire."

"I bet it was that bitch, Jessica!" Usian shouted. "That bitch had been leaving crazy messages on my phone and threatened to do something to Nika."

"Did you tell Nika about it?" Whisper asked.

"We discussed it, but I bought her a gun to use if Jessica came up in there tripping, but I haven't given it to her yet," Usian replied. "I never thought the bitch would set my shit on fire!"

"Do you think she might try to set the house on fire?" Whisper asked, looking spooked.

"I don't know," Usian replied, worried. "I think we need to go to the house to see! CJ, go to the hospital, and I'll be there as soon as I make sure everything is okay at home!"

"Okay," CJ replied, taking off in the other direction.

Usian and Whisper ran down the street and hopped back into the car. It would take them six or seven minutes to get around the corner to the house, but Usian planned on doing it in four. He started up the truck and pulled out into the middle of the street. He couldn't go forward, because other cars were in the way, so he decided to put the truck in reverse and go backward. Usian pulled out into the middle of the street and put the truck in reverse. He put his arm on the back of the passenger seat and looked behind him before they took off. Usian was steady with the wheel, and they were going back smoothly without running into anything. Usian put his foot on the brake to slow himself down before he spun the wheel and sent the truck turning in a semicircle. The police noticed what Usian had done, and one of the police hit his lights. Usian didn't bother stopping when he took off, because he needed to get home.

Usian went down Saint Louis Avenue and turned on Taylor Avenue. He planned on coming down their one-way street the wrong way, and that was going to cut down on their time. He turned onto Bishop L. Scott Avenue and headed west toward Marcus Avenue. When he got to the end of his street, he made a left-hand turn. He was hoping that no cars came down their narrow one-way street, but if it did, he would hit the sidewalk. His truck had good suspension, and that was what those bad boys are made for. Usian got down to the front of their house and noticed a commotion going on. He slammed on breaks and threw the truck in park. Whisper was already out the door before Usian got out and ran up on the sidewalk. He went through the gate and up the pathway but stopped short at the sight he'd seen.

"Ma, are you alright?" Usian asked, breathing heavily.

There were two police trucks that pulled up behind Usian's truck, and a third one stopped in front of it. "Bitch! You're lucky the police are here because if they weren't, I would have beat the shit out of you!"

"I've already done it," Subira said, rolling her eyes. "I tried to yank all of that hair out of her head, but whoever sewed it in there did a good job."

"Moms straight got a machete against this chick's neck," Whisper said, chuckling.

"I tried to cut her hand off, but I got the bottle she was carrying instead," Subira explained. "She was about to firebomb the house and was trying to get into your apartment. You should be able to smell the gasoline all over her. I should have lit a match to her ass and watched her burn. You know my husband used to put tires around people's necks and throw gasoline on them before lighting them on fire. He got the idea from Winnie Mandela when she was fighting over in South Africa. You know my husband has connections with her, but that's a story for another time."

The three police officers walked up to them and looked down at an unconscious Jessica. They moved toward Usian, but Subira lifted the machete and stopped them. "What are you doing? My son isn't the one you should be trying to grab! This woman tried to break into his house and firebomb it!"

"She just burned down my store on Saint Louis Avenue where you followed me from," Usian explained.

"I called for him to get to the house because I had taken down this dumb woman!" Subira explained. "Luckily, I was coming to sit out on the porch like I was telling them. I saw her messing with the screen door, so I eased back upstairs to get my machete."

"Did you cut her, ma'am?" one of the officers asked.

"No, I didn't cut her, but I beat her ass pretty good," Subira replied. "Oh... don't light a match because she's covered in gasoline. The broken bottle she was about to use to firebomb the house is broken into pieces up on the porch.

She thought for a second then looked at Usian. "Where is Nika? She was at the shop, doing hair?"

"I have to get to the hospital because the ambulance was rushing her there," Usian explained. "CJ had to pull her and Jessica out of the shop because this bitch had barricaded the doors."

"We're going to take her into custody," one of the officers reported. "Can you put the machete away so that we can take a report from you?"

"Can whoever's blocking me move their car?" Usian asked urgently. "My wife was rushed to the hospital in the ambulance, and I need to get there right now!"

"I can give you a police escort," the police captain offered.

He was cool with Whisper and provided a little protection around the neighborhood. The one difference about this officer was he grew up in the neighborhood and already knew everyone. It was only right that he protected the people who helped take care of him and his grandmother, so he returned the favor by giving Whisper information about what was going on at the station and who was going to get kicked in or indicted. "My car is the one that's blocking you in, so I'll bag back. The two of you can handle this call. Call an ambulance to come check her out before you bus her ass down to the Justice Center."

"Yes, Captain," the officers replied.

"I'm going to call you after I know what's going on, and I'll send someone to get you," Usian promised.

"I'll call Zaida and have her and Jabari bring me. They went out to dinner and a movie around six this evening, so they should be on their way home," Subira explained. "I'll have them bring me to the hospital, but please call me when you get there."

"Yes, ma'am," Usian replied.

He kissed her on the forehead and hugged her tightly before walking off. He was so worried about his wife and didn't know what to think. He hoped that CJ would call before he made it BJC, but no news might be the best thing for him at this moment.

CHAPTER

*N*ika slowly opened her eyes and blinked slowly. Everything looked a bit blurry, but the lights were blaring down in her face. She breathed in and thought Darth Vader was standing next to her. She reached her hand up, gripping the mask, but she felt Usian's hand grab hers.

"Stop, baby, don't do that," Usian fussed. "It's on your face to help you breath. You were in a fire at the shop. CJ had pull you and—"

"Precious! Where is Precious?" Nika asked, sounding muffled from the mask.

"She's okay, and the baby is okay," Usian assured her. "Allahu Akbar."

Nika pulled the mask off her face and took a deep breath of air. She blew it out slowly, batting her eyes. "Your ass is so hard headed," Usian fussed. "You almost died, woman!"

"But CJ pulled me out," Nika replied softly. "I remember him breaking the window and glass flying everywhere. I had to shield me and Precious's head because she was already on the floor, passed out. I had to drag her from the back because she was stuck in the bathroom. The door was locked, and I had to break it down. My ass is stronger than I thought. I want to thank you for making me do squats."

Usian laughed, rubbing his thumb across her eyebrow. He was so happy that nothing serious happened to her. "Did the fire department say how the fire got started?"

"The stupid bitch Jessica did it," Usian replied angrily. "She poured gasoline over all of the furniture, walls, and floor then lit it on fire. The man who lives across the street from the building saw everything and told CJ what happened."

"Did he tell the police?" Nika asked, frowning. "Why didn't his nosy ass see that bitch barricading the doors? The floor got so hot so quick that it was smoldering under us. I managed to pull Precious close to the door, but I ran out of breath because of the smoke. I wet a towel and tied it around my mouth. I remembered it from a movie we watched." Usian laughed at his wife and kissed her on the head. "The only thing I kept thinking about was *I can't die. I haven't told Usian that I'm pregnant.*"

Usian stared down at Nika with a surprised look on his face. He was so excited that he smashed his lips against hers. Nika pulled away and laughed because she was excited too.

"When did you find out?" Usian asked.

"I found out yesterday when I went to the doctor. I missed my period, so I made an appointment. I'm only four weeks pregnant, and there's a chance I could lose it, so please don't say anything to anyone yet."

"I promise I won't say anything," Usian assured her. "It will be our little secret. Oh shit! I forgot to tell you the rest. Why Whisper suggest we go to the house and check on Ma. I had a feeling that the bitch might try to go to our house and do the same thing, but Ma had the bitch beat up and lying on the ground, knocked on, conscious. She put the machete up to the bitch throat and held it there until the police pulled up. I was so relieved that she was safe."

"Where was Zaida?" Nika asked, looking at him strangely.

"She was gone on a date with Jabari," Usian replied, smiling.

"You so silly," Nika said, laughing. "This is their third date. Jabari has accompanied Zaida to study sessions with her and my mother, and they went out to dinner afterward. She can marry a man outside our religion, you know."

"I know, but it sounds strange, saying that Jabari is going after an older woman. Kimmie has Mac's head all gone. They're moving in together, and he's stressing me the fuck out."

"Why? How do you even have time to be around Mac? You work most of the day, and when you're not at the furniture store, you're at the lounge with Whisper."

"You sound like I don't spend any time with you," Usian said defensively. "I make sweet love to you morning, noon, and night. I've made breakfast in bed for you every Sunday for the past month, and I bought you a house next door to your mother."

"You're the best husband a wife could ever ask for, bae, but you spend a lot of time away from home, and we don't do other people's domestic issues. The only thing we do is give a listening ear and thank Allah that we're not in that situation, okay?"

"Okay, baby," Usian replied, smiling.

CJ walked into the room with a smile on his face. His baby was spared, and Precious was going to be okay. He wanted to make sure that Nika was okay because if it wasn't for her, then Precious and the baby would have been dead. "The man of the hour!"

CJ walked over to the side of Nika's bed and smiled at her. He leaned over, kissing her forehead before he touched the side of her face.

"I owe so much to you, Auntie. Because of you, my baby will have a chance at life," CJ said sincerely. "Man, I'm so glad my uncle married you! You've been down with me and Precious from the jump, and that means a lot to me."

"I appreciated you helping my mother when I moved out. I still owe you for saving her life," Nika countered. "Besides, you are my nephew, and I have to help look out for you. Dealing with you is giving me practice for our baby."

Nika touched her stomach and smiled.

"Nika, you're pregnant?" CJ asked, surprised.

"Yeah, buddy! My wife is pregnant with our first child," Usian announced. "But I'm not supposed to tell people, so don't go shooting off your mouth."

"I won't say shit. I'll let y'all tell everybody," CJ assured him.

"Speaking of shooting off your mouth. Can you tell me why your fingerprints are on the door of a house that had a dead nigga in it?" Usian questioned. "And before you offer a lie, I'm going to advise you not to do it. Detective Smitty already ran some shit down to me, and they're looking to question you about it."

"Damn, Unc. That's fucked up! Pooh was already dead when we slid up in there," CJ explained.

"Who is we?" Usian asked.

"Me and Trey. Trey has a tracker on Pooh's phone, and we used it to find the nigga. I was going to take care of his ass once and for all, but apparently, someone got to him first."

"Did you know that Pooh had dealings with Roc?" Usian asked curiously.

"Nope," CJ replied. "It fucked me up when I saw him come out of the house."

CJ explained to Usian and Nika what happened when he called Pooh's phone. Also, he told them how he and Trey snuck up in the house and found Pooh dead. He said Pooh was naked and looked like someone had beat him to death. Usian advised him to go down to the station to holla at Detective Smitty. He offered to go with CJ if he needed the extra support. Usian also advised CJ that they would bring his lawyer along to make sure no bullshit was involved. He knew that if a solid lead didn't present itself, CJ could be taking the rap for a murder he didn't commit.

"I'm glad someone else did the dirty work for us. Karma is real, and she's a bitch. That hoe ass nigga deserved a much worse death, but his ass is dead either way," Usian said, shaking his head.

"I swear I didn't kill him, Unc. I was going in the house with the intent to kill him, but like I said, the deed was already done. I never told you that Pooh was the one who killed my mama. I saw him shoot her out the car when it happened. He was trying to come for me, but she was on the side-walk. I never told you this, because I wanted to handle him instead of you. I hope you're not mad at me," CJ confessed.

"Why would I be mad at you for wanting to avenge your mother's death? I'm proud that you wanted to handle it this way because you know how I do shit," Usian replied.

"Listen at your super tough ass," Nika added, pushing Usian in the arm. "You always talking about what you would do or what you gon' do."

"You saw me beat that nigga Roc's ass, didn't you?" Usian gloated. "I wish you would have seen when I knocked that nigga out on the gas station parking lot with one punch!"

"I wish I would have seen it," Nika added, laughing. "I would have spit in that nigga's face."

Usian and CJ laughed. "I still believe Roc's ass was the one behind the attempted abduction."

"I believe he was too, but he didn't act alone. CJ dotted the i's and crossed the t's when he said Roc had Pooh's phone. I believe Roc was the one who killed Pooh."

"I could see that too because Carlos doesn't seem like the type who would kill anyone," Nika said, sitting up in the bed.

"Are you okay?" Usian asked.

"Yeah, I'm okay," Nika replied. "I'm ready to go home though."

"Let me go find the doctor so I can see what's up. I'm ready to get you home so I can love you up," Usian said, moving the hair out of her face. "I'll be right back."

Usian walked out of the room to see what he could find out. Nika and CJ talked about what happened at the fire, and he told her about what the old man said. CJ got a text from Precious, so he had to go back to her room. He thanked Nika again for helping save his girlfriend's life, then he left out the room. There were so many thoughts swirling around in his head. He had to go talk to the detectives, and things didn't look good.

Usian brought Nika home and ran her a hot bath. The doctor at the hospital wanted to keep Precious there overnight for observation as a precaution, so CJ opted to stay with her. Usian told him that they would go downtown to speak to Smitty in the morning, but if it was too uncomfortable for him, Usian would have Smitty come to the house so that they could talk. The issue needed to be dealt with as soon as possible because they couldn't afford to have the police sniffing around their house.

"Come on and get in the tub," Usian ordered. "And take your hair down out of that ponytail."

"Okay, bae," Nika replied, yawning.

"You tired, baby?"

"A little," she replied, walking past him. "You smell good."

"You smell smoky," Usian joked. "I took a shower before I ran your water. I'm about to bathe you, wash your hair, feed you, and put your ass to bed."

He was shirtless with a pair of pajama pants on. He put lotion on his chest and torso to moisturize his skin like he always did. It didn't make sense to put it on his arms because they were about to be submerged in water.

"That sounds amazing because I'm tired," Nika whined. "I almost died, and it was scary as hell."

Tears filled Nika's eyes, and her voice started trembling. "There was so much smoke... and I couldn't breathe or see. I... I... I..."

"Sssshhhh," Usian cooed, wrapping his arms around her. "Baby, you're safe now. I don't know what it feels like to be in that situation, but from what I've heard from you and CJ, you kicked ass, Mrs. Simpson."

Nika continued to sob in his arms. She was feeling overwhelmed due to the fact that she almost lost their baby before she even got a chance to experience being pregnant, and for a few minutes, she seemed inconsolable. Usian began to undress his wife because he knew the bath would do her some good. He took off her shirt and stopped to wipe some of her tears, but it didn't do any good. He unfastened her bra, sliding it off her arms; then he pulled her pants and underwear down.

"Step out of your pants, baby," Usian instructed and Nika did what he asked.

Nika wiped away her tears, but they continued to fall. He swept her off her feet and kissed her lips softly as he carried her into the bathroom. He put her down in the hot water, and she sank down into it as if she were melting. Usian pulled up a stool next to the tub that he kept in the corner and sat down on it. He reached over and grabbed a cup, dipping it down into the water. He poured it over Nika's hair as she held her head back, letting it run down her back. It felt so good to Nika as a sigh escaped her lips. Usian did it again one more time, making sure her hair was completely wet. He poured shampoo into his hands and applied it to her long, thick curls, smoothing it out all over it. He massaged her scalp and scrubbed her hair while Nika stared blankly at the wall. Her tears managed to stop falling because she felt safe and secure there with the love of her life.

Usian rinsed the shampoo thoroughly out of her hair before washing it again. He dried it off with a towel before applying some conditioner on her mane. Next, he washed her body until there was no trace of soot on her skin. Nika was appreciative to Usian for taking good care of her. She felt relaxed and was ready for bed. The only thing Nika wanted to do next was climb up in the bed and lay in Usian's arms until she fell asleep.

Usian told her to get out of the tub and she did so. He wiped her off with a soft, cotton bath blanket, and then they went into their bedroom where he slathered lotion all over her body. He sat on the edge of the bed and studied her closely while he rubbed the Shea butter and coconut oil blend into her skin. Nika yawned several times, and that let Usian know that his wife was truly exhausted. He thought about how he would have gone crazy if anything happened to Nika, and to find out she was pregnant made him even more upset about the dumb bitch Jessica's actions. This ordeal was over, but he would make sure the bitch Jessica paid for what she did.

Subira had come downstairs when Nika and Usian first arrived home. She hugged her daughter for what seemed like forever because she was so grateful that her daughter was okay. Subira cooked dinner for them while Nika told her what happened because by the time she was about to leave for the hospital, Usian called and told her that they were about to release Nika. She made one of her daughter's favorite dishes, and the chicken pot pie was the type of comfort food she needed. Subira thanked Allah a thousand times for saving her baby girl. Nika was everything to Subira, and if she would have died, the family would have had to bury Subira right next to her daughter.

CHAPTER

Sixteen

"$\mathcal{L}$et's get this over with, Smitty. I have to get back home to my wife," Usian said dryly. "She was pretty messed up from being in that fire, and I need to be at home with her to make sure she's straight."

"I heard what happened, and I'm sorry that you lost your store. I guess you were about to go legit, huh?" Smitty replied sarcastically.

"I've been legit ever since I got out of prison. I'm a contracted carpenter in a union and everything. I can come work on yo' shit if you need me to."

"I may hold you up on that," Smitty replied, chuckling.

CJ was sitting nervously in the waiting area while Usian talked with Detective Smith. The attorney that Usian had on retainer was on a phone call, so they were waiting for him to finish. CJ didn't know what to expect from the conversation, but he hoped that they didn't arrest him for a murder he didn't commit.

"I'm ready, Usian," Ares said, walking up to the men.

Aries was a good friend of Usian and also his attorney. Ares was the one who represented Usian in his previous case and managed to get his sentence knocked down to ten years, considering the judge was working with the prosecuting attorney. Ares was one of the best criminal defense attorneys in Saint Louis, and he was on Big Lee's payroll as well. "Smitty, this won't take long because my client is innocent, so let's get this show on the road because I'm due in court in an hour."

"Don't come rushing me now, Ares. You're the one who was on a phone call. Detective Jackson is waiting for us in one of the rooms," Smitty replied. "It's this way."

The men followed Smitty to one of the interrogation rooms, but he stopped Usian at the door. "This is where you wait, Usian," Smitty said, pointing to some chairs that were against the wall.

"No problem," Usian replied, pulling his phone out of his pocket. "I'll call and check on my wife while y'all talk."

Usian walked over to one of the chairs and sat down while the other men walked into the room. He knew that CJ was going to come out of this without any charges being filed. Ares was present to make sure that Smitty and Detective Jackson didn't railroad his nephew into a false confession because Smitty was known for doing shit like that to people. Usian hoped that CJ learned a lesson from all of this bullshit. The street life really wasn't for his nephew, and Usian was going to try his best to convince CJ to take a different route.

Roc and Carlos were sitting on the couch, watching television. Roc's father refused to take any of his calls or pay his tuition so he could finish medical school. Roc was still pissed at Carlos for outing him to his father, but for right now, Roc was the only person he had to depend on. He wanted to call Jumba to ask for help, but he was sure that his godfather would take the same stance as Baraka. Baraka and Jumba hadn't been on good terms lately, but Roc knew that it didn't matter. He was committing one of the worst sins that a person could do, and Roc felt that his father would never forgive him for it.

"I'm hungry," Carlos said before snorting a line off the table. "We should go out to eat somewhere good."

He snorted another line up the other nostril while Roc stared at him in disgust.

"I'm not hungry," Roc replied, taking a drink from a fifth of gin. "I don't want to leave the house, so if you want to go out to eat, by all means."

"Why are you being this way?" Carlos asked. "You shouldn't be here beating yourself up like this. We can be together freely now. You don't have to hide in the shadows from your family anymore. Let's celebrate!"

Roc cut his eyes at Carlos. He wanted to hit him upside his head with the gin bottle, but he didn't want to waste the liquor. "You know I love you, Roc, and we'll figure this shit out together."

Carlos attempted to lean over and give Roc a kiss, but he turned his head. "You don't want to kiss me?" Carlos asked, gasping. "You can't stay mad at me forever."

"You can't tell me what the fuck I can and can't do," Roc snapped. "You've completely fucked my life up, and now you're pretending like you haven't done shit! It's you who got all of our money stolen. It was you who brought that bogus ass gangster into both of our lives, and he wasn't good for shit but some good head and ass. Pooh managed to fuck up everything that we asked him to do, and come to find out, he was the one who robbed us. Great job, Carlos!"

"I didn't know any of that shit, so you're not being fair," Carlos rebutted. "Pooh was here for my entertainment. You had your precious little fiancée and me, so I don't understand why you were fucking Pooh anyway, and behind my back, I might add."

Roc looked over at Carlos, unamused. Carlos was well aware that Roc was going to be interested in Pooh because Pooh was exactly the type of nigga that Roc liked. Roc felt like Carlos started messing with Pooh to get back at him anyway, but none of that mattered now.

"How was I fucking Pooh behind your back when all three of us were in bed together several times? I saw how you would stare jealously at us when I was driving my dick deep inside of Pooh," Roc gloated. "The problem is you could never have me the way that you wanted, so you went out of your way to sabotage me every chance you got!"

"Wait a muthafuckin minute!" Carlos shouted, jumping up. "You're not going to blame me for all of this shit! You were the one who went to Pooh about kidnapping Usian, which was a stupid ass idea, by the way! Who kidnaps a drug dealer that's known for being and running with a bunch of killers? Nika wouldn't have married your ass if you would have gotten away with it anyway! It was obvious she was in love with Usian and not you... She didn't even let you hit that, and y'all had been going out for years! Did you even know what her pussy smelled like?" Carlos asked, smiling smugly.

"Fuck you, Carlos!" Roc yelled angrily. "I hate yo' bitch ass!"

"So, nigga! I don't give a fuck!" Carlos shot back. "Fuck you!"

Roc sat on the couch, staring at Carlos vehemently. He took a long drink from the gin bottle he was holding while trying to calm himself down. He needed Carlos in order to have a place to stay, so it would be best for him to be quiet before Carlos got it in his mind to put Roc out.

Ding-dong!

Both men looked at the door then at each other.

"Are you expecting company?" Roc questioned.

"Are you?" Carlos asked, mocking Roc.

He walked over to the window and peeked out of the curtain. "Ah shit!" Carlos uttered. "The detectives are here, and there's two police cars out front too! Hurry up and clean off the table!"

"I'm not cleaning shit off," Roc replied.

"Carlos... open the door!" a voice said from behind the door.

Boom! Boom! Boom! "I know that you're up in there!"

Carlos ran over to the table and began to sweep the cocaine that was sprawled over the table into his hand. He poured it into a cup and carried it over to the bookshelf. He hid it in between two books and pulled an award he'd received in front of it. Next, he checked the rest of the house before going over to the door. He looked back at Roc, who didn't seem to be phased by the fact that the police were at the door. Carlos took a deep breath then another before opening up the door.

"Detectives... good afternoon," Carlos said, smiling nervously. "How can I help you?"

"Is Paki here?" Detective Jackson asked. "And before you lie, his father said that we could find him here."

Carlos looked at the detective in shock.

"I wasn't going to lie and say he wasn't here," Carlos replied quickly. "I was about to invite you in because Roc is sitting on my couch. Why don't you come inside?"

Both Detective Jackson and Smith came inside of the house, followed by four other policemen.

"We have a search warrant to check your house," Detective Smith announced. "Paki... there you are! We have a warrant for your arrest because you murdered Pooh."

"I ain't killed no Pooh!" Roc protested. "That nigga hit his head on the toilet, and that's how his ass died."

"If that was the case, you would have called us as soon as the incident happened. Instead, you took Pooh's phone and left the house for a while before Carlos called the police. The bruising on your knuckles was consistent with the marks on Pooh's face."

"But Roc didn't kill Pooh!" Carlos insisted. "I saw Pooh lying on the floor after it happened. Roc was on his knees next to the body, giving Pooh CPR."

"I'm glad you're so willing to give out information because you're under arrest as well for being an accessory to murder," Detective Jackson said, smirking. "I guess this lover's triangle became too much for y'all. Did you kill him in a jealous rage, Paki? You didn't like seeing Carlos involved with another man, so you decided to beat Pooh to death? Did you catch them in bed together?"

Roc didn't say anything. He lifted the bottle of gin to his lips and took a drink.

"That's absurd!" Carlos protested. "Roc was well aware that I was involved with Pooh. Roc and I have an open relationship, and Roc was engaged to be married a few months ago."

"So I was told," Detective Smitty replied.

"I have something," one of the police said, walking toward the detectives.

He held up an android phone that was in a duffle bag. "I found it in a bag located in the bedroom."

"Whose bag was this phone in?" Detective Jackson asked, studying both men.

"It was in my bag," Roc replied. "It belonged to Pooh."

"Shut up!" Carlos demanded. "We need to call a lawyer."

"I don't need a lawyer," Roc said, standing. "I killed Pooh. We got into a fight, and I was beating his ass. I gave him an upper cut to the chin, and he slipped on the rug, hitting his head on the toilet. I tried to do CPR to revive him, but he was basically dead. Carlos came into the bathroom after the fact and was about to call the ambulance, but I panicked. I convinced him not to call, and we left the house so that I could clear my head. When we got back to the house, the door was open, so that's when we decided to say someone broke into the house. Carlos didn't have anything to do with it… It was all me."

There was a hurt expression on Carlos's face because he knew that Roc was going to prison for a long time. "Carlos, I love you, but fuck you for bringing that bitch ass nigga into our lives! Don't try to contact me, and stay the fuck away! I'm ready if you're going to arrest me."

Everyone stood silent for a few minutes because they were all stunned from the confession. Detective Jackson walked up to Roc and put his hand on his shoulder.

"Thank you for making it easy on us. Officer, please come and arrest this man," Detective Jackson said, taking the bottle from Roc. "Carlos, you're going down too as an accessory, and we'll take what Roc said into consideration when I talk to the prosecuting attorney."

Neither men said a word as the police officers put handcuffs on them. They both knew that jail time was evident, and when another officer came into the room with a bag full of dope, Carlos knew that his fate had been sealed as well. There were ten keys of heroine with several pill bottles filled with capsules ready to distribute. The police escorted the two men to their squad cars and put them inside. Both men were to be taken down to the Justice Center to be booked for their various charges.

TWO WEEKS LATER...

"Hello," Usian said, walking off from Nika.

"It's done," Whisper replied. "Have a good evening, bruh."

"You do the same, bruh," Usian said, disconnecting the call.

He walked back over to Nika and wrapped his arms around her waist. He kissed her on the shoulder and nestled his face into her neck. "Did I tell you I love you today?" Usian asked, squeezing her.

Nika turned around to face him.

"You told me several times when you had me pinned against the wall this morning, serving me that vitamin D," Nika replied coyly. "I love you, baby, and I can't wait to move into our house."

"I can't wait either."

"Who was that on the phone? That was a short conversation."

"It was nothing really, baby," he replied. "Let's get ready to go to the park."

"Okay," Nika replied, smiling. "Let me go grab my bag of snacks so we can go."

Usian watched as Nika disappeared down the hall. He was happy that she was able to get past what had happened to her two weeks ago. She was having trouble sleeping for the first few days, and it tore Usian a part. She didn't even want to have sex, so he knew she was deeply affected. He had a conversation with Whisper about the situation and mentioned how he wanted to fuck Jessica up. Whisper said he had a solution to Usian's problem and told him that he'd get back with him. "I'm ready to go, bae," Nika said, coming down the hallway.

"Okay," Usian replied, grabbing her hand when she walked up to him.

He gave her a kiss and smiled. "Before I forget, I have a surprise for you."

"Oh yeah? What is it?" Nika asked curiously.

"We don't have to worry about the bitch Jessica anymore," Usian said nonchalantly.

"What do you mean?" Nika asked curiously.

"They found her hanging in the bathroom at the Workhouse Medium Security Prison this morning," Usian explained. Whisper had told him previously how Jessica's fate was going to be sealed, so he already knew what had happened. "I guess she couldn't handle what was about to happen to her when she got to court, so she killed herself. At any rate, we don't have to worry about that bitch no more, so you can relax and stop worrying."

"Worrying? Worrying about what?" Nika asked, frowning.

"You can quit worrying about me killing the bitch because she took the initiative and did it herself," Usian replied in a matter-of-fact tone. "That was Whisper on the phone, and he told me."

Nika turned her lips up at Usian before she crossed her arms in front of her body defensively. She knew good and well if Whisper was the one doing the informing, both of those niggas had something to do with it. "Baby, I swear I had nothing to do with it."

"You know what, baby? Fuck that bitch," Nika stated frankly. "We have Allah to thank for our good health and prosperity. That's one less problem we have to worry about, and now we don't have to go to court either. I just want you to know that I love you madly, Usian Jasper Simpson Jr."

"I love you, Amanika Simpson," Usian replied, smiling.

He pulled Nika into his arms and kissed her passionately. She wrapped her arms around his neck and slid her tongue in his mouth as they kissed passionately. They had a long life ahead of them with nothing but peace, love, and blessings.

The End

Six Months Later...

*U*sian and Nika had settled into their new house. It was a bit rough, having the remodeling done while they lived in the house, but they survived. Nika was well into her pregnancy, and her stomach was big as a basketball. She and Usian were so much in love, and people marveled at how attentive Usian was to his wife. Nika was braiding hair at Meme's shop, while Usian and the men who worked at his new construction company put the building back together. They bought the adjoining buildings and planned on gutting them out to make a place for Usian to make and store furniture by the store.

Nika surprised Usian by purchasing him another building, trucks, and all the equipment he would need to start the construction company. She was determined to get her husband out of the streets, but Usian had already put a plan in place and was done the following month after the store was set on fire. Whisper was sad to see his friend exit stage left again, but he was happy for him as well because Usian was genuinely happy with his life. They hung out every day and did things with their wives. Everyone was so excited about them having a son and couldn't wait for him to grow up to play with their children. Usian planned on making a legacy to pass down to all of his children and grandchildren, inshallah.

CJ and Precious were enjoying their daughter, and life was great. CJ had started school and worked for his uncle at his construction company. He managed the office and helped solidify contracts with customers. He had a real flare for business, and it was a good thing since he was going to school for business management. Precious was starting nursing school in the spring, and Granny Subira was going to watch the baby for them for free.

She was so happy that an extended family was developed out of the union of Usian and Nika. She had distanced herself from her oldest sister, Usia, and the other sisters didn't have much to do with her either. Jumba was still being abusive toward Usia, but it was more mental than physical because Usian paid him a visit one night after he left the hospital. Usian told Jumba if he ever put his hands on Usia again, he was going to come up missing. Usian blacked Jumba's eye as a warning, and he took heed. Jumba was well aware of what Usian had done to Roc, so he knew better than to go against the grain.

Roc's charges were reduced to manslaughter, but he faced other charges for trying to cover up Pooh's death. Carlos was pissed off that he was implemented in this entire mess, so he told the police that Roc was the one who bought the drugs. He made it seem like Roc was a heavy hitter, and he was merely his flunky. It didn't do any good, because they both got twenty years for the drugs on top of the years they received for Pooh's death. The two men hadn't seen or spoken to one another since they were arrested, but once they got to diagnostics, it was inevitable that they would meet. Roc attacked Carlos and beat him so bad that he spent several days in the infirmary while Roc had to do thirty days in the hole. Roc's family disowned him, but Adisa was sneaking to see him behind Baraka's back. She couldn't turn her back on their firstborn, and she would continue to support him until she took her last breath.

Jabari fell in love with Zaida the first day they met. He was intrigued by her wisdom, her faithfulness to Allah, and her beauty. Zaida had agreed to go out with Jabari, but after their third date, she told him that she wasn't comfortable with doing so, because she was very attracted to him. She told him that they could remain friends, but the only thing she could do was see him casually at family dinners or other social events.

This hurt Jabari's feelings, but he was determined to make Zaida change her mind. He converted to Islam a month later, and they were married two months after that. Subira bought the house on the other side of her two-family flat as a wedding gift to them, and they settled in shortly after Usian and his workers made some renovations on it. Life was good for everyone, and they all planned to live long, prosperous lives.

CONNECT WITH THE AUTHOR

Website: Vivian Blue, The Author
Amazon Author's Page:
Author Vivian Blue
Facebook Likes Page:
Author Vivian Blue

f facebook.com/VivianBlue

🐦 twitter.com/VivBlueAuthor

📷 instagram.com/Authorvivianblue

ALSO BY VIVIAN BLUE

Royalty Publishing House is now accepting manuscripts from aspiring or experienced urban romance authors!

WHAT MAY PLACE YOU ABOVE THE REST:

Heroes who are the ultimate book bae: strong-willed, maybe a little rough around the edges but willing to risk it all for the woman he loves.

Heroines who are the ultimate match: the girl next door type, not perfect - has her faults but is still a decent person. One who is willing to risk it all for the man she loves.

The rest is up to you! Just be creative, think out of the box, keep it sexy and intriguing!

If you'd like to join the Royal family, send us the first 15K words (60 pages) of your completed manuscript to submissions@royaltypublishing-house.com

LIKE OUR PAGE!

Be sure to <u>LIKE</u> our Royalty Publishing House page on Facebook!

CPSIA information can be obtained
at www.ICGtesting.com
Printed in the USA
LVHW042021040319
609437LV00004BA/335/P

9 781796 933550